GIDEON

The Boy Who Learned to Lead

D1319789

j
F
BAT

Battle, Gerald N.

Gideon- The Boy Who Learned
to Lead

GIDEON

The Boy Who Learned to Lead

Gerald N. Battle

illustrated by
Dorothy Teichman

Word Books, Publisher
Waco, Texas

GIDEON
The Boy Who Learned to Lead
by Gerald N. Battle

Copyright © 1971 by Word, Incorporated
Waco, Texas 76703.

Library of Congress Catalog Card Number: 78-144367
Printed in the United States of America

For Dick

who knows about younger brothers

Contents

About This Book

The Old Testament of the Bible is made up of many different books. There are books dealing with the special laws of the Hebrew people. Other books tell about early Hebrew history in lands we now call Israel, Egypt, Lebanon, Jordan, Syria, and Saudi Arabia.

Other exciting books bring us hero stories told by the Hebrew people. These books are not intended to be factual history. Their purpose is to bring out the basic truth the writer is trying to emphasize. The Book of Judges is just such a book. The writer is trying to say that God, Yahweh as they called him, had not been left behind on Mount Sinai. He was with the Hebrews through all their wanderings. He was with them still in Canaan. Here he would call new leaders to guide them in time of trouble, as he had provided Abraham, Moses, and Joshua in other times.

9

Among the new leaders would be names such as Deborah, Gideon, Samson, and others. Some would be called great, and their names never forgotten. These leaders were often known as "Judges." The title, as it was used then, did not mean a person elected or appointed to preside over a court of law. In the language of the Old Testament the word for Judge was "Shophet." It meant one who sets things right—a deliverer.

When the Hebrew people entered Canaan, after years of desert wandering, they were a nomadic people—people who moved from place to place with their flocks. At last the twelve tribes of Israel settled in one place—Canaan. They built homes. From the Canaanites they learned to plant crops and to farm. The Israelites, as they were known, even adopted the Canaanite Phoenician alphabet. Despite the warnings given by Moses and Joshua, they took Canaanite women as their wives and began to follow some Canaanite customs.

They saw their Canaanite neighbors build altars to the local gods, Baal and Astarte, to insure the fertility of crops and herds. The Israelites also began to build altars to the Canaanite gods. While Yahweh remained the one true God, the Israelites became careless and inattentive about their duty to Yahweh. Whenever they began to forget Yahweh, trouble soon followed.

After each period of trouble and oppression, a leader rose up to free the Israelites and lead them again to Yahweh. These are the leaders the storyteller in the Book of Judges is telling us about. One of the most famous leaders or "Judges" was named Gideon. Biblical scholars do not know

10

the dates of his birth and death with certainty. He could have been born about 1174 B.C., and he might have died around 1114 B.C. We do know he lived most of his life in and near Ophrah. While the exact location of Ophrah is unknown, it surely was not far from the ancient city of Shechem. Many believe Ophrah may have been located between Shechem and Thebez, near the Spring of Far‘ah where the Wadi Far‘ah* winds eastward to the Jordan River.

In the following chapters, you will read what life may have been like for a boy growing up in the land of Manasseh west of the Jordan. The time was more than eleven hundred years before the birth of Christ. The boy in this story is called Gideon. We cannot *know* that any of these things happened to the Gideon of the Book of Judges. They could have happened to *some* boy in that place and time—even to a boy named Gideon, who grew up to be a leader of his people.

Wadi is the Arabic word for a streambed or watercourse. In Palestine for most of the year the streams are dry.

1

Black Tents across the Jordan

Up the winding dry bed of the wadi the man came. Sweat dripped from his forehead and back. Naked to the waist, he ran in long, rhythmic strides, carefully avoiding the stones in his path. In the time of the rains this wadi would be a raging torrent. Now it was a dry creek bed, an open gateway to the lands of the Manasseh tribe. The wadi began to broaden out and the sides, steep in some places, flattened to meet the small plain ahead.

The runner could see his goal. With a great effort he managed to increase his speed. When he reached the third house of the group clustering the flat open space, he fell at the doorway gasping for breath.

"Father," he called, "the Black Tents are coming!"

He had breath for no more words. Already his father, a

tall, bearded man, was bending over him. The older man cradled the young runner's head in his arms and lifted a jar of cool water to his son's lips.

"Speak no more until you have rested a little, Lok my son. In the meantime I will make the necessary preparations."

Joash turned back into the house. The young runner was breathing more regularly now. He stood up while he drank from the water jar, draining all the water in great gulps. Then he leaned on the door frame and spoke again to those inside.

"It was by chance I happened on the camp of the Black Tents, after dark. They were feasting and reveling on the day's spoils stolen from the Gadites. As soon as I saw the black tents in the firelight, I knew they were Midianites. I started home at once. They will not leave before noon so we have a little time, but only a little. Those cursed camels travel like the wind and do not stop for water."

Joash, followed by his wife, Leah, and their youngest son, came out of the house dragging two heavy sacks of grain. His wife carried a waterskin and a smaller sack. Joash lifted one of the sacks to his shoulder and spoke to the small boy.

"Gideon, run as fast as you can to where your brother Caleb tends the sheep. You know the way. Tell him to go to the fields and warn the others of the coming of the Black Tents. Then you must take the sheep up to the cave. We will meet you there. Now, go!"

Gideon started to speak but changed his mind. He turned and soon his legs were flying in the direction of Mount Ebal looming high in the distance. His bare feet kicked up dust

15

as the short skirt of his brown and white striped cloak flew out behind.

Lok, the runner who had brought the news, picked up the other sack of grain and swung it to his shoulder. He was ready to go again with his father. Joash led the way. His wife followed, the waterskin slung across her shoulder. Lok, the eldest son, came last. His quick steps showed no sign of his having run for hours to bring the news of the dreaded Black Tents. The family was headed for a cave in the side of Mount Ebal a few miles away. Here they would hide the precious seed grain they carried. Without seed for another crop, the whole clan would face starvation.

The Midianites were known as the Black Tents because of the tents of black cloth woven from goat hair they used for shelter. They would go through the land of the Manasseh like a plague of locusts. When they had stolen all the harvest they could eat and had grazed their swift camels in the fields of the grain still standing, they would move on through the valley. Only such small stores as were kept hidden would be left for the people of Manasseh.

This year the Midianites had raided earlier than usual. The wheat was not yet ripened. The barley, which ripened earlier, was nearly harvested. These fierce desert warriors came from the lands east of the Jordan and south of the Dead Sea. Year after year at harvest time they struck. Sometimes their desert kinsmen, the Amalekites, raided with them. They raided and pillaged and then rode off, back to their desert. Their camels moved swiftly, covered great distances, and carried heavy loads without the need to stop often for water.

16

Not only the lands of Manasseh were ravaged. The tribes of Gad, Ephraim, and Issachar suffered from the desert raiders. Sometimes, the half-tribe of Manasseh east of the Jordan felt the blow of the Midianites as well. Occasionally, other Israelite tribes in the southern part of Palestine were raided, but the people of Manasseh west of the Jordan could count on yearly attacks. The Wadi Far'ah—dry during the harvest time—made a perfect roadway into the heart of the tribal lands.

Ophrah, village of the Abiezrite clan of the Manasseh tribe, lay just beyond the point where the wadi entered the open plain among the rolling hills. Close by, the Spring of Far'ah seldom lacked water and the crops were very good. For these reasons the Midianites made this land their favorite target for raids. The people of Manasseh were farmers. Each year they worked hard to gather and hide their grain before the desert warriors made their unwelcome visit.

Over in the foothills of Mount Ebal, Caleb was watching the sheep. He was alert to even quiet sounds, for this was harvest season—the time when the raiders might come for sheep as well as grain. In the distance he could see a figure coming toward him. He strained his eyes to see who it might be. It was too small for his brother Lok or his father. Could it be Gideon, so far from home and by himself?

Yes, as the small figure came closer, he could see more clearly it most certainly was his brother Gideon. Now they were within shouting distance of each other.

"Ho, small brother! Is that really you I see? Can it be my brother Gideon, so far from home with no protector?" Caleb smiled as he shouted the words. Something important

17

must have happened to bring his younger brother this distance alone. Gideon was not a lad who liked adventuring. But now the boy stood before him, trying to catch his breath as he spoke.

"Our father wants you to warn the people in the fields! The Black Tents are coming! Lok brought the news." Gideon managed to get the words out even though he was panting from his long run.

"And who's to look after the sheep if I leave them?" asked Caleb.

"Father told me to take the flock on to the cave. He, Lok, and Mother are bringing the seed grain to hide it in the cave." Gideon looked up at his older brother.

"*You,* look after the sheep by yourself? *You,* take them to the cave? You've never been out of sight of our house by yourself before! Do you really think you can do it, Gideon? Won't you be afraid, like last time? You remember when I went to look for a stray lamb—you left the sheep and came running after me?" Caleb spoke gently, but there was no mistaking the doubt in his voice.

Gideon looked down at his toes. Standing on one foot, he drew a circle with the other in the dust of the path.

He did not look up as he answered his brother. "I will do it, Caleb. I'm sure I remember how to reach the cave. Please, Father said I must."

Caleb turned aside to pick up the trailing rope halter of the donkey grazing nearby. He came back to his brother and handed him his shepherd's staff. It was twice the height of the younger brother. Caleb smiled again as he spoke. "I'll be off now. I leave the sheep with you, Gideon."

As he mounted the donkey, he turned for a last look.

"Caleb," called Gideon, running after him, the long staff over his shoulder, "go back the way I came instead of cutting straight down to the fields. That way you will meet Father with Lok and Mother. They may not be able to move fast enough carrying the grain. And you will never be able to warn all the people by yourself. When you meet Father and Lok, put the sacks of grain on the donkey. Mother can lead the donkey to the cave. Then you, Father, and Lok can each go in a different direction to warn the people."

Caleb's face lit up with pleasure at the words of his brother. "That's a good plan, Gideon. For so small a brother you have a better head than any of us." Caleb waved good-bye and dug his heels into the ribs of the donkey.

Still a long way from their goal, Joash and Lok were having a difficult time. The grain sacks were heavy, and it was hard to keep moving as fast as they needed to go. If only they had more time! Just another hour or two would make a difference. None of the three exchanged a word. Every bit of strength was needed to carry the loads on their shoulders. Occasionally Leah turned to look behind her. So far there was nothing to see, but each time she turned she was half afraid to look. The telltale dust cloud would be the first warning sign of the camels of the Black Tents. If only there was time enough!

There was uneasiness, too, among the sheep in Caleb's flock. They knew a strange voice was calling them, and they were restless at the sound of it. The lead ram tossed his head uneasily. Where was the voice he knew? Why the need to climb higher this early in the season when the grass below

19

was still so thick and green? He moved from side to side, swinging his great head in impatience. Still, wherever he turned, there was the small persistent figure calling his name and urging him back into line. Gradually he became accustomed to the thin, high voice so different from Caleb's deeper bass. As the leader settled down, the flock became less restless. Abruptly the climb became steeper, winding between outcroppings of rock.

Anxiously Gideon shaded his eyes from the sun to look beyond the flock. He must not lose his way. They were in deep grass now with no path to follow. At this level the rains were more abundant so that the grass grew quickly over old paths and hid them from sight.

Gideon ran ahead to lay his hand on the shoulder of the old lead ram and stop the flock. He had to make sure of the way. He had made the trip to the cave three times before, but always with his brothers or his father and mother. He had never come alone. Gideon was afraid. The truth was he couldn't be sure which way he should turn. He recognized the great boulder up ahead and knew he must turn either to the right or the left to reach the cave. The wrong turn might lead the sheep into a steep drop-off from which there would be no turning back. He leaned on his tall shepherd's staff and thought for a moment. There was only one thing to do.

"On, Father Abraham," he called softly, using the name his father had given the lead ram. "Guide us to the cave we seek. You have been there many more times than I. Surely you remember the way."

Gideon dropped back to the end of the line. His heart thumped against his ribs.

Father Abraham led the flock steadily on without hesitating. He turned and the flock followed, moving to the left of the boulder. A lamb strayed to munch on a patch of particularly inviting grass. Gideon waved the wanderer back toward the flock.

Had he done the right thing? Soon he would know. Even now he could see Father Abraham leading the first of the flock onto a broad level ledge, about seven or eight feet wide. Now all the flock was on the shelf which stretched thirty feet before narrowing at the far end.

The lead ram circled back to the center of the flock. The others followed in a milling circle, eating the thick, green grass contentedly. Gideon ran to the center of the ledge where a bush was growing straight up against the side of the mountain. Just behind and to one side of the bush was a pile of tree limbs and branches. Unless you looked closely, it appeared to be a dead tree that had been uprooted by a storm and had rolled down the mountainside to lodge behind the bush. Quickly pulling with all his strength, the boy dragged loose a good-sized branch, and then another. Another branch came free and still another. Finally, a large opening appeared in the face of the cliff. It was large enough for a full-grown man to enter by stooping.

Gideon and his flock did not have to bend their heads. The lead ram took the flock into the cave and stood by the entrance. He would be the last of the flock to enter and, of course, the first out again. Gideon pulled handfuls of grass and, holding up the skirt of his tunic, carried as much into the cave as he could. The first two handfuls were for his special friend. Father Abraham munched contentedly.

Walking outside to look down from the ledge, Gideon could see a long dust cloud rising in an advancing line. The Black Tents were coming! He shivered, though the day was not cold. If only the others would come—if only they would come.

2

Sound the Alarm

Caleb knew he must hurry. But the donkey was not happy at leaving the good grass for a wild downhill trot. Always before, this donkey had proceeded at a leisurely pace, following the sheep and carrying the small load of supplies. Occasionally he had carried a lamb or two when they grew tired. And once he had been made to carry a full-grown sheep with an injured leg. The donkey hadn't liked *that* at all! However, those things were part of the routine to which he was accustomed. Now this was different.

Nevertheless, the hard heels of Caleb continued to bang into his ribs. There was no choice. The donkey broke into a steady trot, swinging his head from side to side, ears flopping indignantly. At least it was downhill.

They had reached the foothills and were almost on the

plain. Caleb was becoming anxious. How much longer could it be, he wondered, before he would meet his people? He, too, had seen the dust clouds rising in the east. He urged the donkey on at a faster pace. The path turned sharply, and there he found his father and brother, with his mother, resting briefly. Before Caleb could open his mouth, the angry words of his father reached him.

"What are *you* doing here? Didn't Gideon find you with my message? Don't tell me that boy couldn't find you! His ears will buzz like a hive full of bees when he feels the weight of my hand."

Caleb held up his hand and jumped off the donkey, answering the angry words of his father with his usual smile. "It is because of Gideon I am here, Father. He gave me your message and added a plan out of his own thinking. Help me tie the sacks of grain on the donkey. He'll bear them easily to the cave and more quickly than you and Lok can carry them. Mother can lead the donkey there. The three of us can go in different directions to sound the alarm. Isn't that a good plan to come from your youngest son's small head?"

"I misjudged the lad." Joash, his annoyance gone, regretted the harsh words uttered under the stress of anxiety. "It is a very good plan. One I should have thought of myself, had I my wits about me. The news of these cursed Midianites made me think only of the safety of the seed grain for our village."

Joash had turned the donkey to face again the climb up Mount Ebal. Lok finished adjusting the ropes carefully so the precious sacks were well balanced and would not slip. Joash turned to his wife for a final word before parting.

24

"There is always the chance we may not be able to win our way back to the cave. If all goes well we will be there after nightfall. You proceed there directly. Make no fire and wait for us. Should anything happen to us, you will know what must be done."

He clasped his wife's right hand in both of his, looked into her face for a moment, and turned to give directions to his sons.

First to Lok, the eldest, almost a man grown at sixteen. A tall boy with long legs and the supple grace of a natural athlete, Lok was the swiftest runner, the best hunter, one of the best fighting men of the Abiezrite clan. With bow and arrow, sling, or spear, Lok seldom missed any mark at which he aimed. He talked little and preferred hunting to farming or tending the sheep. He had been on a hunting trip when chance had brought him past the camp of the Black Tents. Casting spear and clothes aside, he had run to bring word of the coming attack. In his heart burned a fierce resentment at these almost yearly raids. Lok rarely expressed his feeling, but secretly he was ashamed that the men of his clan and of all the Manasseh tribe did not stand and fight.

Why must they run and hide in caves? Better to fight, no matter what the cost. His father was chief of the Abiezrite clan and yet he ran to hide in a cave! Lok knew his father was not a timid man. He couldn't understand why he did not fight the Midianites. Someday, he often told himself—someday he'd strike a blow against the men of Midian.

"Go to the fields west of the village, Lok. Those are the most distant and you are the fastest runner. Tell the people

25

there not to return to their homes. The Black Tents will be there before they can return. Warn each to go to his hiding place directly from the fields. As usual they must send one of their number to the next village to pass the word." Joash embraced his eldest son and watched him disappear, running quickly toward the sun.

Now Joash turned to his second son, Caleb. At fifteen, a year younger than Lok, Caleb was shorter and broader. His shoulders and arms were already beginning to show the power to come. While Lok was the swift runner and skillful hunter, Caleb was the farmer whose strong arms and clever fingers made the vines produce the best grapes. It was Caleb who could feel the earth and, letting the soil trickle through his fingers, suggest which crop to plant and the best time for planting. Where Lok was silent, Caleb had much to say. Like his older brother, he was almost a man and, by the standards of that day, already of fighting age should the need arise.

Caleb sought no quarrel, but he never backed down in a fight. While he had no fierce desire to fight the Midianites, he wondered why his father and the elders of the tribe let the Black Tents raid without resistance. The thought of camels trampling and feeding in the barley fields angered him. The slaughter of sheep to feed the bellies of these plunderers, who planted no crops of their own, caused his usually cheerful face to frown. He listened intently to his father's directions.

"Go straight across the valley to the north, Caleb. Warn the people there and tell them to send runners to warn the people of Issachar as well. Hurry now, we've not much time. I will return to the village to make sure no one remains there. Each of us will take whatever safe route he can find back to the cave."

Joash turned and clasped the shoulder of Caleb. In a moment father and son were gone on their separate missions.

As he turned toward his village, the heart of Joash was heavy. He was no longer as young as he once had been. Still, he ran easily and without even breathing heavily. Why had the God of Abraham, Moses, and Joshua deserted them now? Did Yahweh dwell only in Sinai? Here in this land they had won from the Canaanites had Yahweh forgotten his people? Troubled thoughts ran through Joash's mind. Without even a glance, he passed the tall altar of Baal and the wooden pole of Astarte, looming up across from his own house.

In the meantime, up the winding way of the mountain, Leah tugged wearily at the rope halter, for the donkey balked again at carrying the heavy load. The donkey felt he had been tricked. Just when he had resigned himself to leaving the best grass for a trot downhill at a pace faster than he cared to go, his predicament had worsened. Now it was uphill all the way, with a heavier load than he had ever carried. Each time he dropped his head to snatch a mouthful of grass, the rope pulled at his head. At last he gave up. There was no help for it. Steadily the woman walked ahead, tugging on the halter. At last the donkey walked behind without pulling back. He seemed to sense the need to move quickly. Bit by bit they climbed as the sun sank lower in the sky.

Even though he had the longest distance to travel, Lok was the first to shout the warning to people working in the fields. In the first field to the west, eight men cut barley with sickles, while three boys stacked the sheaves in bundles.

"The Black Tents are coming! Even now they may be in the village. Take what you can and go to your safe places. It is my father's word I pass on to you. He has alerted the village." Lok spoke quickly and ran on to reach the next group. He was thirsty, but there was no time to seek water. Perhaps the next group would be able to spare him a swallow.

In the next field, where three men were working with their wives, the grain was almost harvested. Only the peah, the share for the gleaners, was left untouched. (The poor who owned no land were allowed to glean in the corners of the field so that each person had a share in the harvest.) After shouting his news, Lok paused to catch his breath and ask for a drink from the waterskin resting in the shade of an oak tree near the edge of the field. As he finished drinking, one of the men came up to him and began talking.

"Three years in a row the Midianites have struck our village and taken the best of our harvest! Are we always to skulk in the caves of Ebal and Gerizim like cowards, afraid to defend ourselves?" The short, thickset man was red with anger. He could not get the words out fast enough.

"Your father is chief of the clan, but he seems to have no heart to take a stand. Tell him, Lok—tell him we go to our hiding place this time. There's nothing else to do for now. But soon we must either take a stand or give up this land and find a place where we can keep what we grow. What's the use to toil in the fields to feed Midianite stomachs? Tell your father these are the words of Nathan. And there are others who believe as I do."

28

Lok made no reply but nodded his head and started running toward the next field.

To the north, Caleb worked his way steadily from one group to the next, repeating the words of his father. At the last group he reminded them to send one of their number to the neighboring tribe of Issachar to pass the warning. Already he could see behind him the dust cloud which marked the entrance of the Black Tents into the village. He would not be able to return the way he had come. The only way to Mount Ebal and the safety of the cave would be to work his way around the village to the west. It would not be easy in the dark, but fortunately he knew the way well. And now the sun was almost gone.

At the cave Gideon waited and worried. He had no way of knowing whether or not Caleb had reached his father safely. If Caleb had met his father, would his father listen to the plan? Probably if Caleb had a chance to explain the plan his father would consider it. His father's concern for the safety of the village would make him want to reach as many of the people as quickly as possible. But would all three of them be able to find their way back to the cave? The Midianites were cruel warriors and, while their main objective was food and such valuables as they could haul off, they would not hesitate to deal harshly with anyone who stood in their way.

Leaving the old ram to guard the cave entrance, Gideon decided to move down the mountain. Perhaps he could catch a glimpse of his mother. If she were coming with the donkey, as he had suggested, she might be tired and need help. He looked back once to make sure Father Abraham was still at the entrance to the cave keeping the restless sheep secure. Then he began moving down the mountain, already half in shadow.

In the village, Joash ran quickly from house to house, making sure all the women and children not working in the fields had left for a safe place. Each family had a hiding place where they went to escape the raids of the Black Tents. There they kept stored a few necessities and small food supplies. During this season when the danger of raids was ever present, these hiding places were always ready. Each member of every family knew the quickest way to get to his own.

In the last house on the western end of the village Joash found an old man sleeping. Too old to work, the old man slept while his sons, their wives, and children worked in the fields. Joash woke the old man hastily.

"Joel, Joel—wake up. The Black Tents will be here soon. You cannot stay." The old man looked at him sleepily.

"Eh, what? Why do you wake me?" Joel rubbed his eyes.

"The Black Tents—the Midianites are on their way. They'll be here soon," said Joash, helping the old man to his feet. "You must come with me. I'll take you to our cave. Your sons are in the fields. They will not be able to return for you."

At last old Joel understood. He shuffled along as fast as his old legs would take him. Sometimes he leaned on Joash. They had just left the village behind them when they heard the shouts of the Midianites entering their village.

30

Joash wiped the sweat from his brow. The old man might not have been harmed, but he would have been badly frightened. To wake up in the middle of a Midianite raid would have been a frightening experience for a man much younger than Joel. And there was always the chance that, without intent to kill him, the rough play of the desert men might have badly injured the old man. In a few minutes the curtain of night would give them the cover they needed. Far in the distance Joash could see the dim bulk of Mount Ebal. At this moment it looked very far away.

It was a relief for the wife of Joash to see a familiar landmark. The great boulder rising straight up like a huge granite finger lay straight ahead. This was the place she knew. Now it would not be long before she and this stubborn beast she led would be in the cave. Leah's heart beat more calmly knowing that she had come the right way. The seed would be saved! So much depended on it. To the Midianites these sacks of grain would only be food to be eaten or wasted but to the village of Ophrah they meant the difference between plenty and perhaps nothing at all. True, there were sacks of grain in other caves. But this was the best. Each year the best grain was saved for seed for the very best fields so that the crop might improve from year to year. The seed grain had to be saved!

As Leah looked ahead her keen eyes caught a sudden movement by the side of the boulder. There had been just the flicker of light and shadow. It came so quickly she would never have seen it had she not been looking straight at the huge bulk of the rock. What was she to do? Could some Midianite warrior have spotted them from below and climbed up the other side to cut them off? The heart so calm a moment ago raced wildly now. She carried no weapons. On the donkey were the sacks of grain, the waterskin, and a padded jar in which a lump or two of charcoal still smoldered. The staff she used to climb with would be no protection from a Midianite warrior. She looked down, and at her feet lay a stone the size of both her hands. She picked it up. She must move on the grass as lightly as a feather and use the stone as a surprise weapon. Pulling the donkey to one side in a patch of knee-high grass, she let him graze, as if resting for a moment.

Leah dropped quickly to the ground. Quietly she crawled through the grass in a wide circle. The slight ripple in the grass might have been the light breeze skipping down the mountain. If those were desert eyes that watched, they would see nothing.

This way would take her around the boulder and to the rear of it. Everything depended on surprise. There would be just one chance. Could she do it?—the words pounded in her brain as she crawled upward through the grass. The seed grain had to be saved!

3

The Cave

Gideon crouched by the giant rock and stared straight ahead. Why did the donkey graze so carelessly? Where was the figure he had seen earlier in the shadows? He straightened himself for a better look. As he did so a sudden gasp came from behind him. He whirled in fear. Behind him, and perhaps fifteen feet above him, stood his mother. Both arms were raised above her head, her hands clutching the large stone. Slowly her arms lowered and she tossed the stone to one side. She fell to her knees, sobbing.

"Gideon, Gideon, what are you doing here? I might have killed you! Until you stood up I could not tell who it was. I thought it was surely a Midianite ready to leap out. From below I caught only the slightest glimpse of movement. O my son, why did you give me such a fright?"

By now Gideon had recovered his speech. He sat by his mother in the grass as she rocked to and fro on her knees, torn between relief and the shock of what had so nearly happened.

"I left Father Abraham to guard the flock at the entrance of the cave and came back this way to see if you, or the others, were coming. The great rock casts so much shadow I could not see clearly. Then suddenly no one was there at all—only the donkey. That seemed strange to me so I stood up to have a better look." Gideon spoke in a tone more serious than his twelve years seemed to warrant. He looked at his mother as she dried her tears and smiled at him. "I'll fetch the donkey, Mother."

He scrambled down the slope to where the donkey stood, contented at last, eating the grass that grew thickly in this level pocket where the rainwater was caught and held. Together, mother and son climbed to the cave in Mount Ebal. Gideon led the donkey and his mother followed.

Not far from the western outskirts of the village, Joash and Joel rested. They had found shelter in a thorn thicket and waited for the friendly darkness to hide their movements. It would be almost impossible for them to escape the notice of the Midianites this close to the village if they continued in daylight.

Where they lay hidden, a cluster of large rocks was surrounded by brambles and a thorn bush. A small opening provided just enough space for them to crawl in next to the rocks. From their hiding place they heard the shouts of the

Midianites unloading their camels and setting up their tents. House after house was systematically entered and looted. Fires were quickly kindled from charcoal braziers left burning in every house.

Old Joel put his hands to his ears. It sickened him to hear the jubilant shouting of the Black Tents preparing to feast on whatever the village of Ophrah could offer. Joash knelt on his knees and listened. The language of the Midianites was close enough to his own tongue for him to understand what was being said. He had had opportunity enough in any event to become familiar with the Midianite language. This raid was the third in the past four years suffered by the Abiezrite clan. Would it never end? If only they had a leader to bring all the northern tribes together to make a plan! Joash knew he was not the man for that job. Though he had a certain way with words and had managed to get along with the Canaanites well enough—too well some thought—he was not a man others followed. He was chief of the clan because of his great physical strength and cunning, not because of wisdom or character.

Somewhere there would be a leader. But, as always, Joash quickly forgot the future and turned his thoughts to present danger. Soon it would be dark. The Midianites would be sleepy from their feasting and wine drinking. As soon as it was safe, they must start for the cave.

Lok passed the word to the last group working in the farthest fields to the west. He began the long circle back toward Mount Ebal and the safety of the cave. He was careful to

36

avoid the village as he made the swing from west to south. Despite his care, he almost fell into a group of young Midianites as he topped a small hill. Fifteen or twenty men were putting up their tents, but they were so intent on their work they failed to notice the lithe form that quickly dropped to the ground without making a sound.

Lok lay quietly at the crest of the hill, watching the Midianites, most of them no older than himself. They hobbled the camels with short ropes tied around the two front legs. This permitted the animals to graze but kept them from wandering off. As Lok watched, the old anger boiled inside him. If only he had his favorite weapon with him; but he had nothing at all, not even so much as a sling he could put his hand on.

He watched as the tents went up. These Black Tents set up camp in a hurry. You'd have to give them that. The tent poles pulled from the camel packs went up one after another like a well-ordered drill. Nine poles to a large square tent. Three down the middle and three on each side. Each man knew exactly what to do and which position to take. In no time the tents were up and the short pegs being driven in the ground to secure the sides.

Now three more Midianites came in sight. Two of the three carried lambs in their arms. The Black Tents would feast on the lambs of Manasseh this night. Tears of rage came to Lok's eyes. He almost forgot himself and half rose to his knees. Just in time, he came to his senses. He remembered the cave. There were things hidden there he must have, things which would help even the score with these robbers.

Silently he backed down from the crest of the hill. It was almost dark now. He could go around the camp and begin to make his way to the cave. There was something there he ached to have in his hand.

North of the village Caleb had done his job well. He had talked with every group working in that section. He made sure runners were dispatched to warn the neighboring tribes as well as the other villages in Manasseh. Shem, one of the harvesters, with relatives in Issachar, carried the word there.

Caleb was not the swift runner that Lok was, and now as he made his way toward the family hiding place, it was quite dark. The lights of the Midianite campfires made it easy for him to avoid the desert marauders. He could hear their singing a long way off. They sang of their boldness and the fleetness of their camels.

The thought of the hard work gone into this year's harvest—all for nothing now—made Caleb scowl. He loved growing things. Barley, wheat, lentils, the grape vines, and the olive trees—whatever Caleb tended responded to the touch of his hands. It really hurt him to see the camels grazing in the fields of barley, eating the corners left unreaped for the poor. The great beasts trampled as much as they ate. At least they hadn't turned the camels into the fields of unripened wheat, still growing green with the promise of a fine crop in just a few months.

Why did this happen? If Baal, the Canaanite god adopted by the Israelites, made things grow and gave fertility to the soil, why didn't he protect them from the Midianites as well?

The questions stirring in Caleb's head quickened his pace. He was anxious to get to the cave and talk things over with his father and Lok. Perhaps Yahweh, the God of Israel, was the only God who could help. Surely there must be help from somewhere. Tired as he was, he forced himself to move more quickly. Something had to be done.

The warning came from Father Abraham. The old ram got to his feet and tossed his head threateningly. He had heard a sound outside the cave. Gideon, dozing near the entrance to the cave, awoke in an instant. It was pitch black but Gideon knew someone was coming. He bent with his ear to the ground and listened carefully. He heard the footsteps of two persons. Peering out of the black of the cave, his eyes adjusted to the darkness. He could make out a faint outline. Two figures, one leaning heavily on the other, approached the cave. Could one of his brothers, or his father, be hurt?

"Is that you, Father?" Gideon's voice quavered a little with excitement.

"Yes, Gideon. I bring Joel with me. Come, help me."

Joash bent low at the entrance to the cave, and Gideon came quickly to help his father guide Joel into the cave. The old man was exhausted and unable to say a word. Together Joash and Gideon helped Joel back into the cave while Leah unrolled a sleeping mat as fast as she could.

"Light a small lamp now," said Joash. "It will not show from the entrance. Joel's feet are torn and bleeding, and I must bind them up."

Quickly his wife blew on the charcoal in the earthen brazier. She added tufts of dry grass and soon the grass blazed just long enough for her to take the wick from a small lamp half full of olive oil and light it from the flame. By the time she replaced the wick, the grass in the brazier burned out and the charcoal lapsed into glowing coals. But now the lamp, scarcely more than a saucer with a lip, gave a steady light that filled one small corner of the cave.

From her small store of supplies Gideon's mother brought a soft cloth, tore it into strips, and handed them to her husband. He dipped the cloth into the precious supply of olive oil and gently bound the feet of the old man, tossing the sandals with their broken straps aside. Gideon brought a drink of water, cool from the cave. Cheered by all the attention, Joel's eyes brightened and he sat up.

"Thank you, my friends," he said. "You are kind to an old man. My sons and grandsons will repay you for your kindness."

"No need to talk of repayment, Joel. What we have we share. It is the way of our tribe. When Lok comes he will repair the broken straps of your sandals."

Joash moved restlessly about the cave as he spoke. He was worried about his other sons. They were so nearly grown— almost men, but with the quick tempers and untried judgment of youth. He would not be able to rest until they returned safely. To keep himself occupied, he examined the cave he knew so well.

It was a large cave—ten feet wide for most of its length and no less than seven feet at even the narrowest point. The cave ran fifty feet deep into the limestone of Mount Ebal. The ceiling was curved and uneven. Near the center even a man of Joash's height could stand upright, but everywhere else a tall man had to stoop a little. The smooth limestone was easy to cut, and along the sides of the cave shelves had been carved out to form ledges for storage. Dark smudges on the walls and ceiling indicated where lamps were usually placed or fires often built. The cave was warm during the winter, cool in summer, and dry at all seasons.

Joash checked his supplies carefully. There was food enough to last, but the meals would be frugal. There was water enough as well—though, of course, here there was no problem about water. Halfway down the mountain there was a spring which trickled down to the plain below. Joash had never known it to be dry.

They had come to this cave so often; oftener of late than Joash cared to remember. His ancestors had discovered the cave when the Manassites had first come to Canaan. At first it had been a temporary home; a base from which to swoop down and fight the Canaanites off the land below. Later it had been almost forgotten. Then, later still, it had been used as a shepherd's camp during the hot months, when the flocks needed to graze this high for grass and cooler weather. And now these later years, it was as much the family home, it seemed, as the house in Ophrah.

Joash groaned with bitterness and frustration. What *could* he do? He was so lost in his thoughts that Lok was well into the cave before Joash realized his eldest son had returned.

"Lok, you're here at last. Did you see anything of Caleb?" There was both joy and concern in his voice as Joash greeted his son.

"No, Father. All the way here I've seen nothing but those

thieving Midianites. I watched them put up their tents and slaughter two lambs. All the time they howled and sang while they stuffed themselves. Had I so much as a sling with me I would have put one or two of them to rest for good!" Lok spit out the angry words and turned to go searching through the cave.

The words of his eldest son troubled Joash. He knew how hot-tempered Lok was. That hot temper could cause trouble.

"You'll try nothing foolish, Lok? Soon these thieves will be gone. And then we'll be rid of them." Joash followed his son.

"Rid of them? Rid of them until next year you mean! Rid of them till it suits their fancy to come back and steal again! There is only one way to be rid of them and that's to bury them! I'm not the only one who thinks so. Nathan told me to tell you this was the last time he would run to the cave. He's right, you know. We work all year and at harvest we hide in caves while the Black Tents eat our food." This was the longest speech Lok had ever made. All the while he was talking, Lok was feeling around the ledges of the cave and looking behind rocks. At last he found what he was looking for—his bow and arrows.

He took the bow in his arms and stroked it, running his hand up and down the double curve tipped with horn. It was almost five feet from tip to tip—a bow a man could be proud of. There were few Manassites who could boast a bow like this one. It had once belonged to a pharaoh's bowman. The unlucky bowman had been thrown from his horse and killed when his head struck a stone. Lok had happened that way shortly after the unfortunate accident. Finding the bow had seemed like a miracle to him, and in a way it had been

42

a miracle. With the bow and the arrows he had found a different world.

Lok had been a boy of only thirteen when he took the bow and the quiver with six arrows from the dead soldier. His father had made him hide them in the cave, for fear his son would be blamed in the death of an Egyptian soldier. Lok had practiced in secret with the bow more hours than he could remember. At first it had been difficult even to draw the bow. It was a powerful weapon meant to be used by a powerful man.

With persistence that never gave up, Lok had mastered the bow. Now he could place an arrow within a finger's width of where he wanted it, at any range within the bow's striking distance. He had taught himself the craft of arrow-making. No wonder Lok was known as the finest hunter in Manasseh. This silent youth had a weapon which could outdistance spear, javelin, or sling. It was more deadly than the sword or knife. Lok pulled back the bowstring gently, the muscles of his shoulder knotting. The bow felt like a live thing in his hands. He ached to fit the iron-tipped arrows at his side to the bow.

"It would be folly for one man to slay a Midianite or two," said Joash, looking down at his son. "It would only bring open war. They would cut you down and go looking for the rest of us. Our flocks would be slaughtered or carried off, our fields burned. You'll do no foolish thing with that great weapon, my son." Joash, a tall, heavily muscled man, spoke quietly enough but Lok knew he meant what he said. Still, Lok could not give up so easily.

"What one man can do, other men can do. If enough of us

43

kill two or three Midianites our troubles will be over." Lok's tone was as defiant as his words.

Standing in the middle of the cave, Joash rose to his full height, his dark hair brushing the ceiling. He spoke slowly: "I can split the skull of any man in Manasseh in a man-to-man fight. If you think I am old and afraid, you know me not. These Black Tents travel like the wind, and they fight for the love of fighting. To defeat them we need a leader who knows how to make men follow him, a leader who knows how to choose the best men and how to make a plan. It takes wisdom as well as metal to defeat the Midianites and drive them back to their desert lands. We have no beasts to follow them, even if we should win the first battle. Unless *all* the northern tribes fight as one, we will be destroyed. Until we have a leader—a leader with a plan—we'd best hold on to what we have, hard though that may be. To attack them in handfuls, no matter how bravely, is folly. Listen to my words and say no more of this." It was plain Joash would listen to no more arguments from his son.

He had scarcely finished speaking when Caleb came through the entrance of the cave. Joash greeted his second son heartily. The mother hastened to bring water, and now, since all were together, she brought the simple meal they shared. There were a few pieces of barley bread, olives, and nuts.

As they ate Caleb related his experiences. Even his cheerful voice became harsh when he spoke of seeing camels grazing in the fields not fully reaped. Joash held up his hand for the evening blessing. All bowed their heads while he spoke the words:

> "Out of the rock of Moses, the Lord our God
>   gave us help;
> From Egypt he delivered us in ages past.
> He stayed the hand of the enemy.
> He will be our deliverer."

Listening to the words of his father, Caleb was reminded of the question he had wondered about on the journey home. He wanted to ask his father why he prayed to Yahweh and made an altar to Baal. Were two gods better than one? But he was too tired and sleepy to put his questions into words.

"It is time for sleep for all of us," said Joash. "Tomorrow we will talk among ourselves and with some of the others. All that need be said has been said for tonight."

So it was that silence settled over the cave. The lamp was blown out. The faint glow of the charcoal burning in the brazier was a soft red dot in the darkness. Father Abraham settled himself near the entrance. Next to his side, warm and comfortable, Gideon slept.

4

We Were Heroes Then

The early morning sun sent shafts of light into the entrance of the cave. Gideon yawned, stretched, and was suddenly awake. He could hear voices. His father and older brothers talked among themselves. Getting to his feet, Gideon was glad to see his father come to him. There were questions he was eager to ask. But he could see the questions would have to wait. His father was in a hurry and had time only to give him some brief instructions.

"Take the sheep down the mountain, Gideon. There is grass just beyond the large boulder. Graze them there but go no farther. Your brothers and I must talk with some of the others. Return before dark without fail."

Gideon watched Joash make his way stoop-shouldered through the cave entrance with Lok and Caleb following him. It was cool on Mount Ebal in the early morning. Gideon slipped into his cloak, using a short length of rope as a girdle at his waist. Already his mother was bringing him olives and barley bread. Gideon tied the small food parcel to the rope around his waist, then picked up a waterskin and the long shepherd's staff.

"Come on, Father Abraham," he called to the lead ram. "Let's find food for you and your flock." With Gideon in the lead and the ram just behind, the rest of the flock bunched close to their leader. There was still mist in the valleys as the little group made their way slowly down the mountain.

Even before the sun was at its highest the day had turned warm. It would have been easy to fall asleep, but Gideon knew a shepherd must be awake and alert. A shepherd's job held responsibilities. Every lamb, down to the smallest, was important and must be watched over and cared for.

The sound of footsteps aroused Gideon to special vigilance until he caught sight of Joel coming down the mountain behind him. The old man was feeling much better. He could wear sandals on his bandaged feet. And he was walking very well, with the aid of a stout stick.

"I need to feel the sun, so I begged your mother to let me come down to keep you company." Joel seated himself on an outcropping of rock and faced the sun, letting the rays warm his face. Gideon turned to his friend with the questions he had wanted to ask his father earlier.

"What do *you* think we should do, Joel? I know Lok wants to fight the Midianites. Caleb probably feels as Lok does. In a fight people will be killed! What good will it do to fight if many of our people are killed? How can we be sure we would win?"

Joel shook his head as the questions came tumbling out. Gideon looked up at him.

"One can only be *sure* of winning when he knows Yahweh, the one true God, is on his side. There must always be a sign from God. It's true," and Joel shook his head sadly, "in any war some always fall—no matter how just the cause. What should we do? It's a question older heads than yours are asking this day, Gideon. I am old but I have no answer for you. I am so old I can remember stories most of the others have forgotten. I remember the stories my father told me, and his father told him.

"Now, fathers no longer tell these stories to their sons. And, if the fathers forget, how will the sons remember? Ah, Gideon, we were heroes then! We had the courage to dare, for the hand of Yahweh was upon us. And now—now he has forgotten us. Or, could it be, we have forgotten him?"

Joel was silent, and his old eyes looked out across the valleys below and far into the distance. He seemed to be seeing things no one else could see. Gideon came and sat at his feet.

"Tell me of those days you remember, Joel. You said, 'We were heroes then.' Tell me about the days when our people were heroes."

"As I have said, Gideon, I am an old man. The memories of old men stretch back into time itself. It is the fire which warms our bones. Old men have time for remembering and time for talk. So, of course, I'll tell you a story—one worth remembering, though many have forgotten it. This is the story of Joshua and the walls of Jericho.

"Joshua was a very remarkable man. Not as great as Moses, but still a most remarkable man. He had been trained by Moses himself. And to be trained by such a man was a guarantee of greatness to come.

"The time was long ago and long ago. Many years before, our people had come out of Egypt. For years they had wandered in the desert. At last they crossed the Jordan. Joshua had already succeeded Moses as commander of the tribes of Israel. At this time Joshua was an old man but still strong. It was said his voice when he was angry was as loud as the bellow of a young bull. When he spoke the people obeyed. The tribes were camped in a place called Gilgal. This place was only a short distance from Jericho, a strong city with high walls. There was no way the Israelites could advance unless Jericho was taken.

"Joshua sent two men to spy out the land and especially the city of Jericho. The two spies entered the city through the great gates, which were opened during the day but closed at night or in time of danger. The spies found lodging with a woman named Rahab. They made friends with her, and she hid them on the roof of her house. When the king of Jericho heard of the two strangers, he sent soldiers to search for them. Thanks to Rahab the spies were not discovered. Later she helped them escape, letting them out of the window of her house and over the walls with a rope.

"In return for helping them escape, the two men promised Rahab that every member of her family would be spared

50

when the Israelites took the city. They told her to fasten a scarlet thread to the window of her house and to bring all her family inside. Every person in that house would be spared."

"Wait just a minute, Joel," Gideon interrupted, placing his hand on Joel's knee. "I want to hear every word, and I must bring that brown-faced ewe and her lamb back to the flock. Those two always wander off. I'll only be a minute." He jumped up and ran after the ewe, flicking her with his long staff until she turned back to the flock. Then he tossed a pebble at the lamb, who lost no time skittering back to his mother's side. "There! Maybe they'll stay until you finish." Gideon sat down again, and Joel picked up the story where he had left off.

"Joshua was a brave man and an experienced leader, but Jericho was a large, rich city with very high walls. As long as the walls stood firm, the king of Jericho could attack the Israelites with archers and spear throwers placed high on the wall. At the same time he could sneak soldiers out the other side and attack from the rear. The Israelites had to get inside those walls some way!

"One day Joshua walked outside the camp thinking about the problem. He was so deep in his own thoughts he noticed nothing around him. All at once he saw a tall man dressed as a soldier with a drawn sword in his hand. Joshua stepped back, startled.

" 'Are you friend or enemy?' asked Joshua. He was sure he had never seen the man before.

" 'I come as commander of the army of the Lord,' said the man.

"Immediately Joshua threw himself on his knees and

51

asked what was commanded of him. The commander of the army of the Lord told Joshua to take off his shoes, because the place where he stood was a holy place. Joshua removed his sandals at once and his heart was glad. He knew this was a sign from the Lord.

"Bring me some water, Gideon. My throat is dry with so much talking." Joel reached for the waterskin Gideon handed to him. Soon the old man had quenched his thirst and was ready to take up the story again.

First Gideon had some questions to ask. "How could Joshua be *sure* the man who said he was commander of the army of the Lord was truly sent by God? Suppose he had just been a soldier sent out by the king of Jericho to trick Joshua? How could Joshua really know?" demanded Gideon.

"There is no mistaking a messenger of the Lord, Gideon. Joshua knew when God was speaking to him through one of his messengers. No one can mistake the word of the Lord," Joel replied.

"Joshua asked the commander of the army of the Lord what he wanted him to do, and this is what he was told. Each day for six days the army must march around the walls of Jericho. The ark* was to follow the army and behind the ark would follow seven priests blowing seven trumpets made of rams' horns. After the priests came the rear guard, and after them came the people. No one was to utter a sound during the march. Only the priests were to blow their trumpets.

---

*This was the special box in which were kept the stone tablets of the law. It was the special place of God's presence with his people. The description of the ark is given in Exodus 25:10-22.

"On the seventh day all were to march as before, but this day they were to march seven times around the walls of Jericho. After the priests had sounded their seven trumpets for the seventh time, the people were all to shout. If Joshua followed these instructions, the walls of Jericho would fall. Then the army could enter the city and conquer Jericho.

"And it happened just as Joshua had been told. For six days they marched around the walls once each day. The people of Jericho lined the walls and laughed at the strange sight. The only sound from the Israelites was the sound of marching feet and the trumpets of the priests. On the seventh day they marched seven times around the walls of Jericho. The people on the walls shouted insults but received not a word in reply.

"At last the last note of the seven trumpets died away. The seventh march ended. Joshua raised his arm! All of the people shouted with one voice.

"The sound was like all of the thunder from all of the storms that ever were, rolling down from the highest mountain in the world! The very next second the walls of Jericho were flat. Not one stone from those walls touched another stone." Joel's voice rose to a shout. He stood on his feet with his stick raised high like a sword. It seemed to Gideon for a moment that Joel *was* really Joshua watching the walls of Jericho crumble before him.

"And then what happened?" asked Gideon.

"And then . . . and then . . ." Joel repeated the words slowly, still lost in his thoughts. "Then the Israelites entered the city. The people of Jericho and their army were stunned by the collapse of the walls and were easily conquered. All the people and their possessions were destroyed except for the gold and silver which were taken for the treasury of the Lord. The city was burned to ashes. Only Rahab and all her family were spared as had been promised to her."

"I was afraid it would end that way," said Gideon quietly. "I wanted the Israelites to win, but why did so many people have to be killed? I guess it's always that way in a war, isn't it, Joel?"

Old Joel sat down, tired from his long story. "Yes, Gideon, as I've said before, in a war many people are killed." Joel closed his eyes and dozed in the sun.

Gideon walked off to round up the brown-faced ewe and her straying lamb again. Joel's answer hadn't really satisfied him. He still couldn't understand why there always had to be wars.

All the way back to the cave Gideon thought about the story of Joshua. He could almost hear the shrill blasts of the trumpets, the thunder of the people shouting, and the walls crumbling. Just as the last bit of sun left the sky they reached the cave.

On the other side of Mount Ebal different conversations were going on. Joash and his two older sons discussed the situation with their neighbors, who were hiding, like themselves, from the Midianites. Wherever they went the talk was the same. All were unhappy and discontented, but no one knew what to do. Even those most outspoken against the Midianites had no plan of action. They looked down on the valleys below and saw the smoke of the Midianite campfires. They saw camels grazing in the stubbled fields of harvested barley and the black tents of the invaders dotting the plains and hills below. The men of the Abiezrite clan looked down from hiding and muttered to themselves.

Not even Nathan, who vowed he would never run to the caves again, could think of how to get rid of the Black Tents. He and Joash had discussed their problem and found no solution. Joash sent Lok and Caleb on back to the cave while he stayed behind for a last word with Nathan. Now the two men talked about what was really on their minds. Should they leave this land and try to start anew somewhere else?

The more they thought about the idea, the less practical it seemed. This was the place they and their fathers had lived since each of the twelve tribes had been assigned certain lands, with the task of fighting for them and holding them. This was the land their fathers' fathers had fought for and settled on. To leave would make them outcasts. How could they be sure things would be better somewhere else?

As bitter as he was, Nathan realized at last that the answer to their problem must be found here. The land itself was good. Olive trees, gray-green on the hillsides, barley fields, and late ripening fields of wheat proved this land could produce food in plenty. There were vineyards with the grapes already beginning to swell beneath the broad leaves. This was a good land. Somehow they must find a way to protect it.

Wearily, with a heavy heart, Joash made his way back to his own cave. He shouldered his way through the huddle of sheep just inside. Thinking of his unattended fields and the house in Ophrah, he shook his head sadly. He had come home—but it was to a cave!

55

5

To Take a Chance

In the night Gideon was not aware of hearing any sound, but suddenly he was awake. His eyes quickly adjusted to the darkness and soon he could make out objects dimly. Something was wrong! He did not know what. His first thought was to wake Caleb, sleeping next to him.

"Caleb," Gideon called softly. Getting no answer, he stretched out his hand to touch his brother's shoulder. Only the thin woven sleeping mat met his grasp. He crawled over to the mat. Caleb was not there. Now he knew why he had awakened. Caleb had left the cave! No matter how silent the tread, a shepherd awoke instantly when any living thing passed close by as he slept with his flock around him.

Gideon stood up and walked softly out of the cave. There was the faint light of a false dawn. A dark shadow against the gray was barely visible. Was there something moving down the mountain? It must be Caleb!

Gideon darted back to the cave and snatched up his cloak and cap. Quickly he slipped his arms through the short sleeves of the cloak and tied it around his waist. Then he hurried after Caleb. Somehow he must catch up to him and talk with him. He was sure Caleb was going to try something desperate. In his haste he stumbled and almost fell before regaining his footing.

Gideon shivered—not from cold. He was afraid. There was no use telling himself he wasn't. Nevertheless, he had to follow on. He must catch up with Caleb. He could not bear the thought of anything happening to his brother—the brother who always smiled and seldom teased. Caleb understood a younger brother's fears. It was Caleb who had made Gideon's first sling. And it was Caleb who had shown Gideon time after time how to release the thong and send the stone in a straight line. In the end Caleb's patience had borne fruit. The time came when the younger brother could hit a mark at fifty paces, ten straight times without a miss. It was Caleb who had taught Gideon the meaning of every sound and movement of the sheep—something every shepherd must know. Gideon hurried on in the half-light.

Caleb moved boldly down the mountain, unaware that he was being followed. His sling was looped over the leather girdle on his right. His left hand grasped his small cloth bag of specially selected stones. Each stone was almost the same size and each one had sharp edges. The sling was more of a weapon than it appeared to be. A stone hurled from the sling of a skillful thrower could kill at close range if it hit in the right spot. A short knife was thrust through the left side of Caleb's girdle.

Suddenly Caleb paused and looked behind him. It was hard to see against the dark bulk of the mountain, but ears needed no light to pick up sound. Caleb knew now someone was coming behind him. He stepped to one side and slipped the knife from his girdle. Immediately he was hidden in the deeper shadows of a large bush.

Whoever was coming was in a hurry and taking no pains to conceal his footsteps. Presently a figure came dimly in view, drew even, and quickly passed. Caleb thrust his knife back in his girdle and let out a low whistle of surprise. His brother Gideon!

Stepping out from the shadow of the bush, Caleb called, "Gideon, what are you doing here? Have you been following me?"

The shorter figure a few paces ahead stopped suddenly and turned. "Caleb, Caleb, I've caught up with you at last!" There was no hiding the joy in Gideon's voice. He ran back to his brother and threw his arms around him.

"Well, what is this all about? Is there something wrong back at the cave? Did our father send you after me? I thought I'd be well away before the rest of you woke up." Caleb held his younger brother at arm's length and looked into his face.

"I woke up just after you left the cave. When I called to you and got no answer, I tried to wake you up and found you gone." Gideon could never get words out fast enough. "Then

58

when I knew you were gone, I knew I had to come after you. Caleb, you must not attack the Black Tents by yourself. You'll be killed! I know you will! You must wait till our father raises an army." Gideon was fighting to keep the tears from coming.

"Attack the Black Tents? Me?" Caleb began to laugh. He sat down in the grass and laughed harder than ever. "I'm a farmer, Gideon. Our brother Lok is the warrior. I have no notion of attacking the Black Tents. Still, I do plan to do something they may not like. Sit down beside me and I'll tell you about it."

Gideon sat next to his brother. "Yesterday," Caleb told him, "I could see down from the mountain where they'd turned some of those humpbacked beasts into our wheat fields to graze. In two months' time the wheat will be golden ripe and ready to harvest. I helped plant most of it myself. It could be the biggest crop we've ever had!" Caleb pounded the ground angrily with his fist.

"I can't stand by and do nothing while those devils ruin our fields to feed their clumsy beasts. I plan to drive the camels from the wheat fields. That's all, Gideon. I'm no one-man army, nor do I believe our father plans to raise an army." Caleb stood up and prepared to go.

"I'll go with you, Caleb." Gideon was on his feet at the side of his brother.

"No, Gideon. There's not much danger, but something could happen. I plan to steal into the wheat fields, cut the hobbles from the camels, and lead or drive them away. No more than that. Yet something could go wrong. You go back to the cave. I'll tell you about it when I come back." Caleb smiled as he spoke and turned to go.

"I'm going too, Caleb. I want to go with you." Gideon's voice was determined.

"You're only twelve, Gideon, and though you're wiser in some ways than either Lok or I, this isn't your kind of job. I'd better do this alone."

"I intend to go with you, Caleb." Gideon refused to budge.

Caleb shrugged his shoulders. "Come on then. There's no time to waste."

Together the two brothers made their way down the mountain. The coming light was both a help and a worry. Caleb was anxious to be long past the open valley below before the sun rose. The wheat fields lay to the west of Ophrah and there was open ground to cover before reaching them. Hurrying, they came down off the mountain heights into the more gently rolling foothills. There was no sign of anyone stirring. The first rays of the sun sent fingers of light through the sky.

The valley they were entering now ran southeast to northwest, and they worked their way northwest, taking advantage of what sparse cover was available.

Fortunately for the two adventurers, the Midianites had no thought of danger. The guards they posted took their duties lightly. Twice Caleb halted Gideon and placed a finger to his lips. Each time he pointed to one of the desert men sleeping beneath a low bush, sword fallen from his hand, spear on the ground. It would have been easy to kill them as they slept.

Now came the most dangerous part of the journey. Their path brought them within a hundred yards of the village.

Caleb motioned Gideon to stay back while he scouted on ahead. All was clear, and he signaled his brother with a quick wave of his hand Gideon ran to him cautiously, looking on all sides as he ran.

While Caleb and Gideon circled around the village there was a great deal going on in the cave on the mountain. Joash, first to awaken, did not take long to discover two of his sons were gone. Worry and fear made his deep voice rougher than usual, and he shouted with anger. He had guessed immediately what had happened. Caleb was gone on some crazy stunt and Gideon had followed. His first impulse was to send Lok to bring them both back. Lok, the swift runner and keen hunter, could track and catch them more quickly than anyone else. But Lok was much too eager to strike a blow against the Midianites. It would be dangerous to send him alone. It would be better to wait and see. Perhaps Caleb and Gideon were off on some harmless adventure nearby. If they did not return soon, Joash and Lok would both go after them, but for now they would wait.

In the absence of Gideon, Joel offered to take the sheep out to find grass since they needed to be grazed. He felt strong enough to do this, he said. And so it was decided. Joash and Lok would look in the nearby caves for Caleb and Gideon. Joel would take care of the sheep, and Leah would stay at the cave in case Caleb and Gideon returned. If Caleb and Gideon were not found in the area close to the cave, Joash and Lok would go down the mountain to find them.

At last Caleb and Gideon were past the village. A good

thing, too, for now the sun was up. They could see the green of the young wheat fields rising on the rolling plain, perhaps a mile ahead of them. Caleb's mouth tightened at the sight and his jaw thrust slightly forward. Camels grazing in the fields he had helped to prepare and plant!

Gideon stayed close behind, his shorter legs working hard to keep up. The day was getting hot, and perspiration rolled down Gideon's face beneath the round wool cap he wore.

Caleb stopped suddenly, turning quickly to his brother and clapping his hand over the younger boy's mouth to cut off any outcry. With his free hand he pointed ahead. Looking past his brother's outstretched hand, Gideon saw the black tent ahead of them. Both boys dropped to the ground. They were closer to the wheat fields than they had thought. On hands and knees Caleb led the way in a wide circle to the left, where the grass was taller. There was a small clump of trees up ahead of the tent. If they could reach the trees unseen, a sudden dash from there to the wheat fields might take them to temporary safety. The wheat was high enough to hide them once they reached the fields.

The black tent faced the wheat fields at an angle. The best route led through a patch of low bushes behind the tent. If only the Midianites were still sleeping or were occupied inside their tent, the two brothers could carry out Caleb's plan. They had come this far and Caleb was determined not to give up. He looked back at Gideon and smiled encouragement. Gideon tried as hard as he could to smile back, but the smile simply wouldn't come. There was a funny feeling in the pit of his stomach. More than anything else he wished they were back at the cave on Mount Ebal. A lump rose in his throat. He saw Caleb move ahead on hands and knees. Gideon tried to put out a hand to follow, but it seemed rooted to the ground. Finally, with a tremendous effort, Gideon slowly began to follow.

Caleb was leaving him behind. In his haste to catch up, Gideon hit his knee on a stone. He remembered not to cry out, but, angered by his own clumsiness, he picked up the stone and threw it aside. As luck would have it, the thrown stone hit a second one and made a clunking sound. At the sound Caleb turned and motioned Gideon to stretch flat on the ground. A moment later, from the front of the tent a tall, slim Midianite came out and looked toward the wheat fields. Slowly he walked over to the campfire. A few embers still burned in the scooped-out fire hollow ringed by stones. He squatted by the fire and blew. Gradually he added handfuls of dry grass and chips of dried camel dung. The fire burst into flame and slowly the young Midianite strolled back inside the tent.

Moving as quickly and as silently as they could Caleb and Gideon went ahead again on all fours. Fifty yards away the grove of oak trees beckoned them. They knew the Midianites inside the tent were awake. A group of them might come out any minute. Rekindling the fire seemed to indicate some preparation of food might take place outside. If Caleb and Gideon continued their cautious movement on all fours, it might take them too long to reach the trees. If they stood up and ran, the chances of being seen increased.

Caleb made up his mind quickly. This was the time to take a chance. He put his mouth to Gideon's ear and breathed the

63

words of his decision. Gideon was to go first. Caleb pulled the short knife from his girdle and held it in his right hand. To Gideon he gave the sling and bag of stones. Caleb would wait until Gideon reached the trees; then he would make his run.

Gideon's eyes widened as he listened.

Now! Caleb gave the younger boy a shove and watched anxiously as the short legs flew toward the trees. Half-way, three-quarters, only five more yards! As he saw the figure of his brother disappear into the shadow of the trees, he sighed with relief.

Knife in hand, Caleb rose and looked carefully around. He paused for a moment to listen for any sound coming from the tent. It was well he did, for the next instant two Midianite boys came out of the tent and walked toward the fire. Caleb dropped flat again. He judged one of the boys to be his own age. The other was younger, perhaps Gideon's age and about his size. The younger boy seemed richly dressed and wore ear-rings and an amulet on a chain around his neck. His robe was bordered in purple and his headdress was bound with a purple band edged in gold thread. A chief's son, perhaps, thought Caleb. The younger boy returned to the tent. The older stayed by the fire and added some twigs to the flames. A call came from inside the tent. The boy by the fire turned at once and hurried back into the tent.

It must be now or never, Caleb said to himself. Suddenly he was off and running swiftly, but with care, toward the trees. The angle at which the black tent had been pitched placed its front opening toward the wheat fields, but one long side was

64

slanted toward the grove of trees. Just when Caleb was sure he would never reach safety, the shadows of the oak trees came up and swallowed him. He sank to his knees and gulped in the cool air. Gideon looked down at him. He was smiling now. Neither brother spoke but their smiles said everything.

"We're past some of the hardest part, Gideon," Caleb said at last. "We're lucky those Midianites aren't early risers. The day is beginning to warm up and soon they'll lift the sides of their tent for more air. Later on they'll seek the shade of these trees. We'll have to do our business quickly."

"Do you think we can get the camels out of the wheat without being caught? There may be a lot of men inside that tent." Gideon was doubtful.

"Once we get to the wheat fields and run the camels off, we have the advantage, no matter how many men there are. We're used to traveling on foot and we know the land better than they do. Without their camels they'll never catch us." Caleb spoke confidently. For a moment Gideon forgot to be afraid.

"We'll cross the wheat fields the same way as before, Gideon. You go first when I tell you. Then when you're in the fields I'll follow as quickly as I can. But first let me see where the camels are."

Caleb caught a low tree limb and pulled himself into one of the oak trees. Soon he was high in the branches, with a good view of the countryside. At last he saw what he was looking for. A dozen humpbacked shapes were in the far end of the wheat field. This was luck! The animals were at the far end of the field away from the tent. Caleb came down from the tree in a hurry. He walked with Gideon to the edge of the shadows.

"It's about twenty yards across to the fields. This time crouch over and run as fast as you can, but be sure and keep low. Their camp is in a little hollow. There isn't much chance they can see us if we crouch over, even if they look this way. Ready? Now!" said Caleb.

Caleb watched as Gideon, bent almost double and running as fast as he could, disappeared into the green field of young wheat. One quick look at the Midianite camp, and Caleb followed his brother.

There was no time for further rest. Both stooped to stay below the top of the wheat as they scrambled toward the far end of the field. At last, thought Caleb, the goal is in sight. We'll get to those pesky camels and chase them far enough away that it will take those Midianites a while to find them. Maybe then they won't put them in the wheat fields again. They'll know we could have killed the camels instead of chasing them away.

"Hold up, Gideon. We'll stop for a minute and I'll tell you the rest of the plan." Caleb sat back with Gideon beside him. "When we reach the camels, I'll cut the hobbles with my knife. We'll wait until I've cut all the hobbles before we chase the camels out of the fields. If we don't, they'll get excited, and it will make it harder to finish cutting the others loose. Understand?"

Gideon nodded.

"Let's go," said Caleb, raising his eyes just above the level of the wheat to make sure of the direction. He smiled to himself as he thought of chasing the twelve great camels out of the wheat fields. The Midianites certainly would be mad. The one he thought might be a chief's son would really yell at the others.

Caleb grinned. Running crouched over in a wheat field was hot work, but he was beginning to enjoy it. He'd show those Black Tents that men of the Abiezrite clan didn't plant wheat to make a pasture for camels! It wouldn't be long now.

6

Gideon Runs Away

With Caleb in the lead, the two boys crawled through the wheat, moving more cautiously now, for they didn't want to excite the camels by appearing too suddenly. Caleb knew they must show themselves a little before they reached the animals. He paused again to peer above the top of the wheat to see how close they were to the camels. He judged it was time to walk upright. The camels were thirty yards away—twelve of them, a few yards apart from each other. Caleb motioned to Gideon to stand up. They could hear the snuffling noises the camels made as they snatched mouthfuls of the young wheat and chewed them leisurely.

"Just follow me, Gideon. Stay a few feet behind and stop when I tell you to. These animals are used to people. If we do nothing to startle them, they won't pay any attention to us. We're far enough away so the Midianites can't see us. Stay close and do what I tell you."

Knife in hand, Caleb walked slowly toward the nearest camel. A length of rope fell to the ground from the camel's neck. The usual halter had been removed to let the animals feed more easily. Already they had trampled flat a large area of the wheat.

The nearest camel paid no attention as the two boys approached. Peering around Caleb, Gideon saw the length of rope tied between the camel's front legs, just above the ankles. The rope was long enough to allow the beast to move, but he could not run and could only walk slowly.

Caleb grabbed the lead rope and handed it to Gideon. "Hold the end of this rope while I cut the hobbles."

Gideon grasped the very end of the rope, standing as far from the camel as he could. Kneeling at the camel's feet, Caleb quickly found he could untie the knot holding the hobbles in place. With his knife he cut the length of rope in half. It would be too short to use again, something else for the Black Tents to worry about.

Caleb quickly ran over to the next camel while Gideon led the first one. Again Gideon held the lead rope and Caleb went through the same procedure. Now two camels were free of hobbles.

At this point Caleb began to see his original plan wouldn't work. Gideon could handle no more than two camels with the lead ropes. Caleb could handle two more with luck. They would have to get the unhobbled camels out of the field, speed them on their way, and come back to work on the others. It would take much longer than Caleb had planned. He had an idea, but it would depend on Gideon. He knew Gideon didn't like being so close to the camels, but the idea was worth a try.

Caleb took the lead rope of one of the camels from Gideon and stopped, facing his brother. "This is going to take longer than I thought, Gideon. But there's one way we can speed it up, if you're not afraid. Will you try something if I tell you what to do?"

"Tell me what you want first, Caleb. I have to know what you want me to do." Gideon was not going to promise even Caleb without knowing what the promise bound him to.

Caleb sighed, but he knew his brother. "I want you to lead these two camels out of the field. When you get them out, loosen the slip knot on the lead rope of the first camel and pull the rope off. Use the rope to give him a good whack and start him running. Then do the same with the other one. Watch them. If they stop after a little way, use the sling to start them running again. We want to chase them as far away from the wheat fields as we can. Toss the lead ropes into the field where the wheat is high so they'll be hard to find. Can you do it?"

Gideon didn't answer, and his face was solemn. He thought over everything Caleb had told him. At last he nodded his head. "I'll do it. I don't like these camels, but I know we ought to get them out of the wheat fields. Especially since we've come all this way! As soon as I can, I'll come back to you."

"Good," said Caleb. "Go, and be as quick as you can."

70

Caleb turned back toward the other camels. Gideon started through the wheat field, the tip of his head barely showing, the camels plodding behind him. They seemed used to being led.

Gideon stayed as far from the camels as he could. The large beasts frightened him. He'd never been this close to one before and here he was leading two of them. Finally they reached the edge of the field beyond the borders of the wheat. Now came the hard part. To loosen the slip knot Gideon had to stand very close to the camel. He tried to do it with one hand but it just wouldn't work. He dropped one lead rope and put his foot on it, hoping the camel wouldn't pull away.

With both hands free to work on the other rope, he managed to get one end through the loose knot and pull it from the camel's neck. One camel now was completely free. He turned quickly to the other. Soon two camels were free. Standing to one side, he whacked first one camel and then the other with the ropes. The startled animals ran as expected.

As Gideon watched, he saw them slow down and stop twenty yards away. That wouldn't do. He pulled Caleb's sling from the rope at his waist and, loosening the drawstring on the cloth bag of stones, took out two. One he held in his left hand and the other he put in the leather seat of the sling. He wound the end of one thin leather thong twice around his index finger, anchoring it securely. The end of the other thong he held firmly between forefinger and thumb. Around and around his head he whirled the sling, listening

71

to its singing whistle. At just the right moment he released the thong, and the stone sped through the air. Plop! It hit the flank of one camel. Stung by the stone, the animal raced down the valley at full speed. His startled companion shuffled away a few steps, uncertain what to do. Then the second stone hit home, and the second camel raced after the first.

Gideon turned back toward the field, picked up the two lead ropes at his feet, and tossed them into the wheat. He moved as quickly as he could toward the other camels. Caleb must be near one, he knew, but which one he could not be sure. Then Caleb stood up and Gideon saw him. As he drew near, Caleb came toward him leading two camels and smiling.

"You did well, Gideon. I looked up and saw you send those two big fellows running down the valley as if a swarm of bees were after them. Here are two more for you to start on their way."

This time it was easier, for Gideon was less afraid of the camels. He whacked harder with the ropes when he got them out of the field. The camels ran out of sight without stopping.

Even though things were going well, Gideon was worried. He'd be glad when they could start back for the cave. The cave! He wondered what his father and Lok were doing. Who was tending the sheep with Father Abraham? Gideon felt guilty. He realized he shouldn't have gone out without telling his father. He knew his father must be very angry.

Gideon was right when he guessed that his father was angry. But Joash was not just angry; he was worried too.

73

Between them, Lok and Joash had visited every Abiezrite family nearby. They had crisscrossed the mountain seeking word of Caleb and Gideon at every cave. From Machir, Caleb's best friend, came the only clue. Machir told Joash that Caleb had seen the Midianite camels in the wheat fields the day before and had become very angry. He hadn't told Machir of any plans to *do* anything about it, but Caleb had seemed very upset.

Joash and Lok returned to the cave. In his girdle Joash placed a two-edged sword with a blade that measured thirty inches from hand grip to tip. Next to the sword he thrust a short knife. Lok took his knife and his bow with six arrows. They were ready to go. Caleb and Gideon had two hours or more head start, but the older men would travel faster. Joash was determined he would not come back without his two missing sons.

Lok led the way down the mountain. Without the need for concealment, they moved quickly during this part of their journey. The test would come when they left the mountain. To reach the wheat fields in full daylight, avoiding the Midianites, would not be easy. No matter how difficult, they must find Caleb and Gideon. Chances were they needed help, thought Joash.

Gideon had made three trips from where Caleb was unhobbling the camels to the edge of the wheat fields. Half the camels were now free and out of sight. Returning to the open place where the wheat had been trampled and the remaining camels were grazing, Gideon felt uneasy. He didn't know why. Something seemed different. The six remaining camels were there. Caleb was not in sight but he was probably crouching down by one of the camels. Still Gideon couldn't get rid of the feeling that something was wrong.

There were only a few yards between him and the cleared space. Gideon dropped to his knees and crawled through the wheat slowly. When he had almost reached the edge of the trampled area, he stopped and looked through the green stems of wheat waving over his head. There was Caleb sitting on the ground with his legs stretched out in front of him—but he was not alone. Two young Midianites were on either side of him. One Midianite knelt on one knee, holding his knife with the point near Caleb's throat. The other and smaller of the two stood upright, leaning on a slim javelin taller than himself. The metal blade at the end glinted in the sun. In his left hand, he held the lead ropes of two unhobbled camels.

Gideon could see them both plainly. The one leaning on the javelin was richly dressed. The headband of his burnoose was purple brocade. The white tunic he wore was bordered in the same purple brocade with gold threads. He seemed to be looking directly at Gideon. Slowly Gideon backed further into the wheat on hands and knees. He began to crawl to the left slowly in a wide circle. A light breeze moved the wheat above his head and helped conceal his movements. Gideon did not dare to raise his head above the wheat to see how far he had come. He crawled on. It was hot inside the wheat. Gideon's heart beat so loudly he thought surely the Midianites must hear its thumping.

At last he felt he must have come far enough. Cautiously

he raised himself until he could just see over the wheat. He was directly to the side of and forty feet away from the richly dressed Midianite holding the camels. Gideon unloosened the bag of stones from the rope around his waist and selected three stones. He laid the sling on the ground, carefully straightening the thongs and adjusting them. Somehow he had to distract the Midianite holding the knife. Gideon placed two of the stones on the ground next to the sling. The third he held in his right hand. Drawing back his arm he tossed the stone into the wheat exactly opposite the kneeling Midianite.

The slight sound of the falling stone caught the attention of both Midianites. The one with the knife sprang to his feet and looked toward the sound. His back was turned in Gideon's direction. He took two steps toward the far edge of the cleared space and stopped, listening. Gideon stood up. He had to stand on tiptoe to get his arm well above the wheat and to sight on his target. The Midianite holding the camels was his first target. The second stone was for the Midianite whose back was turned toward him. Around and around whirred the sling singing its deadly song. Gideon released the holding thong between thumb and forefinger. Straighter than any arrow the stone sped toward its target. The next second, all was confusion. A camel reared and screamed! The animal broke away and ran wildly, followed by the second camel.

Gideon saw the two Midianites knocked to the ground by the fleeing camels. He didn't quite know what had taken place, but suddenly the weight of everything that had happened closed in on him. The empty sling still in his hand, he turned and fled blindly toward the edge of the wheat field. He knew only that he had to get away from this place—he felt smothered by the wheat. At the edge of the field he instinctively turned back along the way they had come.

Ahead of him Gideon could see the grove of oak trees and, beyond, the black tent of the Midianite camp. His mind told him to take cover in the trees and to approach the grove cautiously in case some of the Midianites were there. But Gideon was not listening to his mind now. His only thought was to run as fast as his legs could carry him toward the safety of Mount Ebal and the cave.

He was abreast of the grove and still running without slackening his pace. A minute more and he would be in full view of the Midianite camp.

Suddenly a figure sprang from the shadows of the grove and grasped Gideon about the waist, lifting him off his feet. In a moment Gideon and his captor disappeared into the grove. Gideon kicked and gasped for breath in a grip that held him like a vise.

Suddenly Gideon thought of Caleb. Caleb had needed him and he had run away! Everything had gone wrong. This was the end.

7

The Javelin in the Wheat

At the foot of the mountain, Joash and Lok were forced to slow down and exercise more care. It was broad daylight now. If they met any of their enemies the Midianites, they might be delayed in saving Caleb and Gideon from capture. They must avoid the Midianites at all costs. So, while Joash and Lok traveled essentially the same route as Caleb and Gideon, they took a wider swing around the village in order to find more cover.

Just as Caleb and Gideon had found the black tent of the Midianites in their path, so Joash and Lok were faced with the same obstacle. The situation was worse for Joash and Lok. Now the sides of the tent had been rolled back to allow air to circulate. Those inside could see clearly in three directions. Only the back of the tent blocked their view.

Scouting off to the left, Lok found a small grassy mound rising just high enough to provide cover for two men stretched at full length. Fortunately it was in line with the back of the tent. Lying behind the mound, Joash and Lok planned hastily. They would have to stay in direct line with the back of the tent and they would have to move swiftly and silently. There was no way they could pass around the tent without being seen. They would have to advance on the tent and capture those inside if they were to reach the wheat fields. There was no other way.

While they planned, they saw two of the Midianites come out of the tent and point toward the wheat fields. The two Midianites talked as they set off in the direction toward which they had pointed. Lok and Joash could hear the sound of their voices, but were too far away to make out what was being said. They were sure the two Midianites were headed for the wheat fields where Caleb and Gideon might be. Joash and Lok would have to hurry. Lying on his back behind the mound, Lok braced his feet against the bow and bent it, testing the pull. Quickly he fitted an arrow. To run holding his bow at half-draw with arrow fitted was a task few men could accomplish, but Lok gave it scarcely a thought. Joash drew his sword. They were ready!

Joash led the way and Lok was at his shoulder. They ran with the quiet swiftness of desperate men. At the back of the tent they paused. Lok drew back his bow to full draw. Sword held high, Joash moved to the right while Lok went to the left. In a moment they were looking in on four very surprised Midianites. The four were seated cross-legged on a woven mat in the center of the large tent. All four were drinking wine, and one was telling a story while the other three listened. Lok's bow, with the iron-tipped arrow at full draw, and the two-edged sword of Joash put an end to the entertainment. In one corner of the tent, camel packs and harnesses were piled high. Curtains which normally divided the tent into separate compartments were pulled aside so that the interior of the tent was entirely open.

In one swift leap Joash moved to the corner of the tent where the camel gear was piled. Pulling out ropes, he cut off four lengths. He ordered the Midianites to come to him one at a time. Quickly he bound the hands of each man behind him while Lok held his bow at the ready. There was much talk but no resistance. When all four Midianites had been tied securely, Joash, carrying more lengths of rope, prodded them into motion with his sword. They needed little urging. With Lok in the lead and Joash following, the group moved quickly toward the grove.

At last Lok could ease the strain from his arm. He took the arrow from the bow and slung the bow across his shoulder. Soon they reached the grove of oaks. Lok and Joash bound each Midianite to a separate tree. From each man they removed his headdress, and then used them as gags. There would be no warning outcries from these fellows. They had just finished with the last Midianite when they heard the sound of someone running. Joash was at the edge of the grove in a flash.

From the opposite direction to the one in which he and Lok had approached the grove, a small boy came running. Joash

80

squinted his eyes against the sun. Yes, it was Gideon, running as fast as his legs would carry him. Something had frightened the boy out of his wits to make him run so carelessly, straight toward the Midianite camp. Joash stepped out from the shadow of the grove. One huge arm reached out and wrapped around Gideon, whirling him off his feet.

Gideon had no idea the arm around his waist was his father's. He thought one of the Midianites had certainly captured him. Once more in the shadow of the oak trees, Joash set his youngest son on his feet. Gideon looked up, too frightened to speak. It was his father! For a moment he could not say a word, and then the words seemed to leap from his throat.

"Caleb is back in the wheat field. Two men have him. We have to go back and save him!"

"Show us the way through the field to Caleb. Hurry, boy!"

Joash and Lok followed Gideon as he ran back the way he had just come. Lok placed an arrow in his bow and Joash had his sword in his hand. If only they were in time. Just as they reached the edge of the field a ripple waved the wheat. Out stepped Caleb, carrying a slim wooden javelin tipped with a metal blade. In his girdle there was a second knife.

Joash ran to meet his son. "Caleb, you're safe!" He flung his arms around his son. "You're safe!" There was pure joy in his voice.

Lok stood silent and smiling. Gideon held back. He had run away when Caleb needed him! Things would never be the same again. Tears filled his eyes so he could scarcely see.

He felt miserable. It was then, staring at the ground, he felt arms around him and looked up to see Caleb hugging him tightly.

"Had it not been for Gideon here, things might not have turned out so well," said Caleb, looking down into his brother's face. He lifted a corner of his tunic and wiped the tears from Gideon's eyes. "It was Gideon's skill with the sling that saved me." Caleb turned to the others, his arm still around his younger brother.

"Tell us about it when we are back at the cave," said Joash. "So far we've been lucky. Now we must hurry. If the Midianites catch us here we may never see Mount Ebal again—any of us." The four turned back the way they had come. Striking off in a wide circle to take them well away from Ophrah, they began the journey back to the cave.

They were tired when they reached the cave, but their luck had held and they had avoided contact with the Midianites. Twice before they reached the safety of the mountain there had been some anxious moments, but at last they were safe. The sparse evening meal of barley bread, olives, and figs was ready to be eaten. Rations had to be stretched when the cave was their home. Joash lifted his hand and his family bowed their heads.

"Blessed art thou, O Yahweh, who has spared our sons and permitted us to eat this food."

All raised their heads and began to eat the simple meal. When they had finished, Joash broke the silence.

"Now, Caleb, tell us all about your adventure. I am anxious to know just what happened." Joash, settling back on his sleeping mat, rested on one elbow. The three sons gathered around him with their mother and Joel.

Caleb began his story.

"Yesterday I could see from the mountain a long way. The air was clear and bright. I looked toward the fields where we had planted the wheat. I was thinking how lucky it was that it would be still awhile before the wheat ripened. Before that time the Black Tents would be gone, and we could harvest our wheat without worry. And then I saw them. I saw them driving a group of camels into the fields to graze on the unripened wheat." Caleb shook his head. Thinking about it made him angry all over again. He pounded a hard fist in the palm of the other hand.

"I felt something had to be done. It seemed best to try it alone. I was afraid Father would not permit me to try it if I told him my plan. Then halfway down the mountain I heard footsteps behind me. It was Gideon. I tried to persuade him to go back, but he would not. So we went on together. You know about the camp of the Midianites. We were earlier than you and Lok and got past the tent without being seen, and on into the fields.

"I unhobbled the camels, two at a time. Then Gideon took those two out of the field and ran them up the valley, while I unhobbled others, and so on. We were half through when suddenly two Midianites came at me through the wheat. My back was turned and they were on me before I knew it. One held a knife at my throat. I couldn't cry out. They were certain I was not alone. They waited without sound.

84

"I was sure Gideon would walk in on them unsuspecting and be caught. There was nothing I could do to warn him. Why he didn't get caught I don't know. Gideon will have to tell you about that. All I know is that one of the two Midianites heard a sound and jumped up and looked toward it. The other held the two camels I had unhobbled.

"All at once one of the camels reared, screaming in pain. Both of them bolted, knocking down the Midianite holding them. When the other Midianite sprang to help his comrade, he was knocked down by the second camel. Lying on the ground, I was unhurt. I saw that the two Midianites had each taken a good knock on the head, so I used the short lengths of rope taken from the hobbles to tie their hands and feet. Then I took their weapons and came out of the wheat to look for Gideon. I knew he must be somewhere near, because just before the camels reared, I had heard the hiss of a sling. I knew my brother was not far away." Caleb smiled at Gideon and put his arm around him, patting him on the shoulder.

"Now, Gideon, tell us your part of the story," said Joash, looking at his youngest son.

Still excited by the closeness of their escape, Gideon began.

"I was coming back to Caleb after taking the camels out of the field and chasing them up the valley. I had nearly reached the edge of the clearing when I felt something was wrong. I didn't know why. I dropped to my knees and decided to crawl the rest of the way. As I got to the edge of the cleared space, I could see through the wheat. There was Caleb lying on the ground with the two Midianites on each side of him. One was kneeling and holding the point of a knife at Caleb's throat. The other held the two camels.

"I decided to back away and try to circle around to the left in order to use the sling without being seen. It wasn't until I had crawled almost to the other side I realized what it was that had warned me. Anyway, I kept crawling until I felt sure I was where I thought I needed to be. Then I took a look. They still hadn't spotted me. I tossed a stone across the cleared space, and the Midianite with the knife jumped up and looked that way. He was still looking with his back to me when I stood up and let go with the sling. I aimed for the Midianite holding the camels. My second shot was for the one with his back to me, and the stone seemed to go straight for him! At the last second, though, one of the camels moved his head in the way and the stone hit the camel in the nose.

"I saw the camels rear and then I was afraid. I was so frightened I couldn't think of anything but getting out of the field! I ran! I didn't even think about Caleb. I was a coward."

Gideon stopped and now there were tears in his eyes. He lowered his head. He couldn't look at his father.

"You were wrong to run, Gideon. Caleb told you not to come with him, but you insisted. When you insisted on going with your brother, you bound yourself to help him in his cause. You *did* help him. Without you, I doubt if eight camels would be running loose now. Without you, your brother might have been captured, or even killed. Lok and I might easily have come too late to help. And I remember your first words to me were of your brother Caleb.

86

"All of us are frightened at times, Gideon. The next time you won't run away. You planned well to toss the stone and distract the Midianite's attention. But I am still curious about one thing. Tell me, what was it that warned you when you were coming back to join Caleb and decided to crawl the last part of the way?" Joash was looking at his youngest son and the smile took some of the gruffness out of his voice.

"Oh," said Gideon, "it was the javelin! The metal tip gave off sparkles in the sun. I must have noticed something was different without realizing what it was. Then while I was crawling to the side, trying to decide what to do, I remembered the point glinting in the sun."

Caleb turned away, only to come back a moment later carrying two things. One was the sling he had started out with that morning; the other was the javelin he had taken from the Midianite. "This one is better than your sling and I want you to have it. I may need you to hit another camel in the nose for me someday. The javelin is light enough for you to throw. I'll keep the knife. This way we'll both have something to remember this day by."

The two brothers smiled at each other, and Gideon's heart was suddenly light again.

8

A Fire Burns on Mount Ebal

The next day the news traveled over the mountain like the wind. Camels of the Black Tents had been chased away from the wheat fields! Six Midianites had been left bound with their own ropes! A dozen men of the Abiezrite clan gathered at the cave of Joash. They sat on the ground and listened as Joash told them the whole adventure. He described the roping of the four Midianites to separate trees and the special satisfaction of gagging them with their own head coverings.

Nathan forgot to frown and slapped his thigh, rolling with laughter. "Maybe that will teach them a lesson. Graze their camels in our wheat fields, will they!" Nathan was happier than he had been for days.

There was even talk of storming down from the mountain to fight the Midianites! The clan was excited and proud of having caused the enemy some discomfort, but Joash soon made them see that one small village could not take action alone. It would take all the men of Manasseh and of the nearby tribes as well acting together if anything was to be done. But nevertheless, spirits were high, and Joash realized that the blow which Caleb and Gideon had struck, small though it was, meant a great deal to Ophrah. Now they could endure their misfortune more patiently.

When Gideon returned with the sheep, visitors were still gathered at the entrance to the cave sitting and talking. Joash encouraged the conversation. He knew how important it was for the people to enjoy to the fullest their feeling of satisfaction at the Midianites' expense. He knew all too well the kind of days which lay ahead. There were fields to be replanted, houses to be repaired and placed in order, tools to be mended, and animals to be rounded up. There would be much to put to rights when the Midianites left. With pride in the successful outcome of Caleb's bold plan still lifting their spirits, the people would set to their tasks of repairing the damages to their homes and fields in much better temper.

Quietly, and without attracting attention, Lok and Caleb went around to the caves nearby. They returned with the wives and children of the men who were gathered around the fire, bringing with them enough of the simple foodstuffs to feed the whole group. For the first time, cooking fires were prepared outside the cave and allowed to show as much light as needed. Joash knew there was little chance the Midianites would climb Mount Ebal this late in their stay. It was easier for them to move on to another village. The desert men preferred open country, and they never fought at night if they could help it.

Gideon's return with the flock was cause for a new outburst of talk. There was much comment about how one small Israelite lad's sling had caused so much confusion to the enemy. The sling Caleb had given Gideon was passed around. The javelin was brought from the cave along with the knife Caleb had taken. Both were passed from hand to hand and examined carefully. Leah enlisted the help of the other women and they passed among the men distributing the thick porridge made of lentils. To add to the festive occasion, there was honey one of the men had found the previous day and brought to share. The children played games and shouted, until their mothers gathered them up and made them sit quietly.

Gideon said nothing, only watched on the outskirts while the men and older youths took part in the conversation. Now he sat beside Joel. A lull in the talk gave him the opportunity to speak out.

"Tell us a story like the one you told me when we were tending the flock the other day, Joel. Remember? You told me about Joshua and the walls of Jericho." Gideon tugged at the sleeve of Joel's tunic.

"Some other time, Gideon. When we tend the sheep again I'll tell you another story. These men don't want to hear an old man's tale of hero days." Joel smiled and looked across the fire at Joash.

"What is this tale of hero days, Joel?" The deep voice of Joash rose above the hum of conversation around the fire.

"Oh, the other day I watched the flock with Gideon. To pass the time, I told him the story my father told me years ago, the story of Joshua and the battle of Jericho. We had heroes in those days, Joash. And we followed Yahweh, our God, and did not bow to Baal. The twelve tribes of Israel did not flinch from any foe." As he answered Joash, Joel's voice grew louder and seemed to take on new strength.

Joash became thoughtful for a moment, and he looked about him. For the first time since the arrival of the Black Tents, the men of Ophrah were less discontented—planning was beginning to take the place of grumbling. Perhaps Joel could help keep their spirits up to face the hard days ahead.

"We have need of heroes now, Joel. Though none of us here are heroes, even plain men can take heart from the deeds of others. Tell us such a story as you have told to Gideon. I promise you we'll listen with keen ears."

Joash motioned to the men to spread out in a circle about Joel. On the outskirts of the circle, mothers held their children close to them.

"You do an old man honor to listen to his tale. But the story is not mine. It is a part of our common heritage—a heritage we must all remember. Here is the story I would tell you; and I tell it to you, as my father told it to me.

"The time was not so long ago, as time is reckoned. The place was as far from here as Jericho, but to the north instead of south where Jericho lies. Our people were occupied with farming. Once we had won our land, we did not establish armies to stand idly by. We worked our land and fought only when forced to fight. There was a king of the Canaanites who lived at Hazor, north of the Sea of Chinnereth. This Jabin, for such the king was called, became very powerful. He grew so strong he forced our people of Naphtali and Zebulon to submit to his rule. Jabin ruled our people with harshness. The men of Naphtali and Zebulon resisted when they could, but there was no strong leader to rally the men of both tribes to fight against Jabin. With his army commander Sisera at the head of a strong army, Jabin held our people beneath his thumb.

"At this time in the hill country of Ephraim, to the south near Bethel, lived a wise woman named Deborah. She was a prophetess, and her talent was so well known that people came from far away to seek her advice. It was Deborah's custom to sit beneath a palm tree near her home and share her wisdom with all who came to her for judgment.

"Deborah had heard of the troubled times at Naphtali and Zebulon. One day she sent a man to summon a certain Barak of Kedesh in the land of the Naphtali. This Barak had proven himself a brave fighter against the tyranny of Jabin.

"From Kedesh to Deborah's home was a two-day journey and not without danger. Even so, Barak came in response to Deborah's call because he had heard of this wise woman and was curious to know why she had summoned him. Deborah did not keep Barak waiting long.

" 'Return to Kedesh, Barak. Raise an army from the men of Naphtali and Zebulon. Do this, and follow the instructions which I will give you, and I prophesy a great victory for your army. You can throw off the yoke of Jabin and free your people.'

"Barak was amazed to hear these words. He could scarcely

believe them. He had fought as a soldier, but Barak had never led an army. And, to tell the truth, he was more farmer than soldier.

"At last Barak agreed to do as Deborah wished, if she would accompany him. Barak was not afraid, but he needed the wisdom of Deborah at his side. Deborah agreed and they returned to Kedesh together. There Barak sent out a call for men. Ten thousand answered.

"Acting on instructions from Deborah, on a certain day Barak marched his men to Mount Tabor. Drawing them well up into the foothills, he made camp and waited. Across the plain from Mount Tabor, the river Kishon glistened in the sun. And Barak waited with his army.

"When King Jabin heard of Barak's army, he ordered Sisera, his commander, to take such men as he needed and to destroy the Israelites. Sisera laughed when he heard of the army encamped on Mount Tabor. He called out nine hundred chariots, drawn by the swiftest horses in the country and manned by the best charioteers in the army. Sisera boasted that the green plain of Esdraelon would turn white with the bones of Barak's army.

"Along the bank of the Kishon River, Sisera drew up his nine hundred iron chariots in long ranks. The plain of Esdraelon lay between the two armies. Sisera planned to race his chariots at full speed across the plain when the Israelites came down from Mount Tabor. According to Sisera's plan, the chariots would cut the foot soldiers of Barak to pieces. Still Barak waited in the foothills. Finally Deborah sent word the hour had come.

"Barak waved his sword high and swung it twice around

his head. Ten thousand men unsheathed their swords. They started down the flanks of Mount Tabor. Suddenly the sky turned black. There was a roll of thunder louder than all the drums of all the pharaohs of Egypt. Ten thousand men charged toward the plain! As the first of Barak's men reached the plain, the rain came from behind them.

"Proud Sisera, still smiling and confident, waited. He wanted to make sure every Israelite was killed. He waited until the last rank reached the plain and there could be no turning back. As fast as stout legs could run, the men of Barak charged across the plain. From behind them the rain came harder, driven by the wind. Rain drove into the eyes of the waiting Canaanites and their horses. Horses reared and were frightened! The plain became a sea of mud.

"At last Sisera gave the signal to attack. But the iron wheels of the chariots spun deep into the mud. Horses could not move. Chariots were overturned. All was confusion. Behind the chariots the river Kishon rose out of its banks and spread a watery trap for the Canaanites. The Israelites on foot could move more quickly than the Canaanites, who were struggling in the mud with their horses and iron chariots. Soon the battle was over. Jabin's army was destroyed and the people of Naphtali and Zebulon were free."

Joel sat back, his story finished. All was quiet for a moment and then Joash spoke.

"A fine story, Joel. And a true one. I heard it long ago, even as you have told it this night. I had almost forgotten it. I wish there were a Deborah here to tell us what to do. We thank you for the story."

"There are those who say," said Joel, slowly and hesitantly, "that it was Yahweh who spoke through Deborah."

No one answered the old man.

Only Gideon looked into Joel's eyes with a question. He would need to think about it. Perhaps tomorrow he would ask Joel about what was on his mind.

"I think we should send out scouts to see if the Midianites are getting ready to move on." It was Nathan speaking now, and there were echoes of agreement around the circle.

"Yes, that may be a good idea, Nathan," Joash agreed. "But only men to scout and report back. We want no hasty action which might delay their leaving! Whom shall we send?"

Lok was the first to speak.

"Send *me*, father! I'm ready to go now or any time." The eldest son of Joash stood up.

"I'll go as well." The voice was that of Jethro, Nathan's son.

"And me," said Machir. "I'll not let Caleb have all the adventures."

"I, too, will go." It was Laban, Joel's grandson, a tall lad of seventeen, who spoke next.

"Four of us will be enough. More will be too many. Let the four of us go," said Lok, still standing.

Joash looked at the four young men. They were four of the finest young men of the Abiezrite clan. Scouting was a young man's job. Speed and agility meant more than strength. He longed to take the risk with them, but these four would be better off without him, and he knew it. With an effort he choked back the words he wanted to speak, the words that would have taken him with the four.

"Agreed," said Joash at last. "The four of you leave at first light. But only to find out the movements of the Midianites. There is to be no fighting! Remember my words! It could be that Yahweh, our God, has not forgotten us. Perhaps the Black Tents are ready to move on."

The four nodded their heads.

Now the gathering broke up, and all began to return to their own caves. Only the four scouts lingered to make plans.

"We'll leave from here at first light," said Lok. "Make sure no one is late. Unless we're off the mountain early, we'll have trouble. Their guards will not be sleeping this time."

The others left and Lok turned toward the cave. Before he lay down on his sleeping mat he checked his bow carefully and placed bow, arrows, and knife in easy reach. Tomorrow could not come too soon. He pulled the bow nearer and was fast asleep.

9

Gideon Takes a Stand

All day the four scouts, Lok, Jethro, Machir, and Laban, had been gone. Since late afternoon the fathers of the four scouts and their friends had waited at the cave of Joash. These were anxious moments. Time and again Joash wondered if he had acted wisely in sending Lok. He knew the resentment against the Black Tents that was burning in Lok's heart. And yet his eldest son *was* the best scout in all the Abiezrite clan. A father had to trust the judgment of his son. So Joash waited, impatiently and with misgivings.

At last Caleb came running and shouting. "They're coming! I saw them. They're coming!"

"Are all four returning?" Joash asked the question quietly, but the nervous movement of his hand betrayed the anxiety he felt.

"Yes, I counted four and then I ran to bring the word."

Caleb's answer brought welcome relief to the small group waiting just outside the cave. Finally the four scouts themselves came in sight—all four were safely back on Mount Ebal. Lok came first with his bow slung across his back. Machir followed, with Jethro and Laban bringing up the rear. After the greetings the four sat down to rest and make their reports. Lok spoke first.

"We came off the mountain in the early morning before there was much light below. Since there were four of us, it seemed well for each to go in a different direction and to meet at the foot of Mount Ebal on our return. If any of us did not return on time, we would know the direction to search.

"I went to the west; Laban to the east. Jethro started with Laban and then turned north. Machir started with me but stayed at the village to watch there until I returned. Then the two of us were to come back together. I learned it took the Black Tents all of yesterday to recapture the camels Caleb and Gideon turned loose. Those camels belonged to the chief of the Midianites and his family. The javelin Caleb took and gave to Gideon belonged to the chief's son. The Midianites were not happy about that.

"From what I could overhear, the main body of the Midianites are going on to raid the villages in the north. A small party will go back down the wadi and return directly to the desert. I do not know why." Lok finished his report.

Machir spoke next. "I went with Lok and stayed at the village while he went on to the west. I crept as near the village as I could without being seen. There was a thicket of

99

thorns on the edge of the village which made a good hiding place. That's where I stayed."

"Oh, yes. I know that place well," interrupted Joash. "Joel and I hid there the first day of the raid."

"Well, I could look out from the thorn thicket and see a good deal of what was going on. Sometimes they came near enough so I could overhear parts of conversations. Their talk is so much like ours I easily understood what they were saying. The women were talking about getting ready to leave. From what they said, I judge they will be leaving tomorrow." Machir turned to Laban.

Laban began to speak. "I went around the village to the east. The main body of the Midianites seemed to be there. From what I overheard they are planning to raid the people of Issachar and go still farther north. Then they will cross the Jordan and come down through the half-tribe of Manasseh east of the Jordan. From there they will move on south to the desert.

"Some of them were angry about the camels' being run off. Others were laughing at those who had been taken by surprise and tied to trees. Like Machir, I feel sure they plan to break camp tomorrow. That's all I learned." Laban turned to Jethro.

"Laban and I were together at first," began Jethro. "Then we reached the point where he continued east and I turned north. There were few Midianites to the north of Ophrah. But those who *were* there seemed to be the advance scouts. Their camels were with them, not grazing with the main herd. They carry few supplies, since they live off the land. I saw a group of ten or twelve, each with a small sack of grain.

100

"I could not get too near, but I am certain these are advance scouts. They are getting ready to leave early tomorrow. I'm sure they are heading north. It seems to me two days from now it should be safe to return to the village. Some of us might go down tomorrow. That's all I learned."

"You have all done well," said Joash. "It's good news you bring us. Soon we can return to the village and our homes. We have already warned the people of Issachar, so they will have made such preparations as they can. They may be able to warn the people east of the Jordan, if the Black Tents plan to pass that way. The Black Tents are leaving none too soon. We are in much need of the pastures down below for our flocks. We will move them there as soon as it is safe."

With these words the group began to break up. Everyone looked forward to the next day. They would soon know if the Black Tents were actually on the move again.

Early the next morning, as soon as the mist had lifted and there was light enough to see below, the people of Ophrah looked down from Mount Ebal. What they saw made them happy. There were only a few of the black tents left. And even as they watched, those tents began to come down. The Midianites were leaving. To the north they could see a long line of camels moving away from the village.

Careful as always, Joash waited until late afternoon and then sent the four scouts back to make sure the village was clear. The four returned just as dark covered the mountain. They reported there were no Midianites in Ophrah. Tomorrow they could start moving back to their homes. Joash sent word to every cave on Mount Ebal—"Tomorrow we return to our homes."

As soon as the sun was high enough the next day for good light, Joash sent Gideon with the flock down the mountain in search of better grass. "Search out some of the good grazing land to the east of the village, Gideon. You'll have to take care of the sheep by yourself. Joel will be helping his sons and grandsons. Lok, Caleb, your mother, and I will have much to do."

It was a happy time for Gideon. They were all going back to Ophrah. The sheep would graze again in familiar pastures. Even Father Abraham seemed to know they were going home. He marched at the head of the flock just behind Gideon. Looped over Gideon's rope girdle was the sling Caleb had given him. Next to it was tied a small bag of selected stones for his sling. It was just like the one he had left in the wheat field when he had fled in panic. In his left hand he carried Caleb's other present to him, the javelin. His right hand carried the shepherd's staff. Slung low on his shoulder was a skin of water.

The sheep moved slowly, and the morning was half spent before they reached the foot of Mount Ebal. Gideon led the way eastward toward his favorite pasture, a small meadow bordering the Wadi Fa'rah. During the season of the rains when the wadi ran high with water, the low bank on the meadow side overflowed and gave this patch of ground more water. For this reason the grass always grew well here. Because it was farther from the village than the other pastures, Gideon usually had this one to himself.

By early afternoon Gideon and the flock reached the good green grass. Keeping one eye on his flock, Gideon set up a fallen branch from an old sycamore tree. He wedged the branch with stones to keep it standing straight. He measured off fifty paces and practiced throwing the javelin. At first he missed the branch by a wide margin, but he kept on practicing. Finally he was within a foot of the branch on nearly every throw. When his arm grew tired, Gideon put the javelin down and turned back to his flock.

Almost immediately he knew something was wrong. One of the lambs was missing! Quickly he circled the sheep into a tight huddle in the center of the meadow. He placed the lead ram on the outside of the huddle of sheep. Taking off his cap, Gideon placed it on top of his shepherd's staff. Then he drove the staff deep into the ground. This would be a marker to guide him. If anyone else came along, it would be a signal that he had gone looking for a stray.

Gideon took the javelin with him. It would serve well in case an animal had attacked his lamb. He went back the way he had come but he found no trace of the missing lamb. Next he went down the low bank on the meadow side of the wadi into the wadi itself. Slowly he clambered up the winding, rock-strewn dry bed of the wadi toward Ophrah.

There was still no sign of the missing lamb. He turned back down the wadi, passing the meadow where his flock huddled. Eastward toward the Jordan he followed the wadi. On the side opposite the meadow the wall of the bank rose fifty feet. On the meadow side the bank was only shoulder high. Gideon's eyes searched the winding course of the dry bed. Tufts of grass grew between the rocks, but there was no indication that a lamb had either nibbled or trampled any of them. He

103

must find that lamb. If he had not practiced with the javelin, he would not have let that lamb out of his sight. A fine shepherd he had been!

He heard the sound and turned but it was too late. There were four Midianites. Two jumped in front of him and two just behind. Plainly, not all the Midianites were gone. Gideon stopped and backed away toward the far bank in order to face all four of the enemy. This time there was no place to run. And now he saw the missing lamb. One of the Midianites carried it in his arms. Gideon's eyes widened in recognition. The one carrying the lamb was the same Midianite who had held the knife next to Caleb's throat in the wheat field. And next to him was the richly dressed Midianite—a boy about his own age and size. The other two were men—young men of sixteen or seventeen.

"That's my lamb you have," said Gideon. "I've been looking for him. He must have strayed. Give him to me." He started toward the older boy, who was holding the lamb. Immediately the two men on his right grabbed his arms and held him tightly.

"*Your* lamb! I'll have his throat slit for my supper. Whatever is here is ours to take and do with as we please. You Manassites hide in caves from the Midianites. How does it happen you aren't hiding in your cave now?" The young, richly dressed Midianite was speaking. The words cut Gideon like a knife. Before he realized he was speaking, he answered.

"We do not always hide in caves, Black Tent. I seem to remember seeing you and the one holding my lamb there,

104

before. Only then you were both lying on the ground in my father's wheat field!" The words had leaped out of Gideon's mouth before he thought. He wished now he could call them back again, but it was too late for that.

"So you were one of those? I thought so when I saw you with my javelin. Release him, Nahash, Balak—and hold the javelin. What do you know about the camels that were released and driven away? Tell me or you'll be in worse trouble yet." The young one Caleb had thought was a chief's son spoke. At once Gideon was released and the javelin wrenched from his grasp.

"My brother Caleb saw your camels grazing in our wheat fields. It angered him, and he started alone to release the camels and drive them out of the wheat. I saw him go, followed, and went with him. My brother unhobbled the camels. I led them from the fields and sent them up the valley with my sling. When I was returning to my brother, I sensed something was wrong. I crawled through the wheat to the place where you held him. I could see the two of you through the wheat, waiting for me. I crawled around to the side and planned to use my sling to hit both you and your companion. Only at the last minute one of your camels moved his head and the stone struck him in the nose instead of hitting you in the head. The camels reared and ran away.

"You were knocked down by the first camel. The second knocked your comrade down. My brother tied up both of you, took your weapons, and left. That's what happened," Gideon finished.

"And where were you while your brother was tying up Hanun and me?" The voice of the richly dressed Midianite was as haughty as ever.

"I—I was afraid and ran away." Gideon bowed his head as he spoke.

"And where did you run without being caught by my people?" the Midianite asked.

"I ran from the wheat field toward your camp, but my father and eldest brother came seeking Caleb and me. They met me. Just as we turned back to help Caleb he came out of the wheat field." Gideon was sure this was the end of him. They would never let him go now, not after hearing all of this.

"So it was your father and brother who sneaked up on my men, captured them, and tied them to trees. We know where your flock is, Manassite. We saw you bring the flock into that meadow and watched you all the while. The lamb strayed near the edge of the wadi while you were showing us how clumsily you throw a javelin. One of my men took the lamb, knowing you would surely follow to look for it. There is nothing to prevent us from killing you and all your sheep as well. It would be just revenge for the sneaking trick you and the others played on us." The boy stopped speaking and looked directly into Gideon's eyes.

A plan formed in Gideon's mind as he spoke. "We could have killed your camels or crippled them back in the wheat fields. We only wanted to get them out of our fields and save the wheat. My father could have killed your four men instead of just tying them up. And Caleb could have killed you

106

and your companion as you lay unconscious, but he only tied you up. If you kill our sheep, our people will never rest until they have revenge. You won't find it so easy the next time you come to Ophrah, if you start by killing me and my flock.

"My father is the chief of the Abiezrite clan. From the way you talk you must be a chief's son. Let's settle this ourselves—just the two of us. Why not wrestle? The one who throws the other two falls out of three is the winner. If you win, you keep the lamb, and I return the javelin. I'll give you my sling as well and show you how to use it. If I win, you return the lamb and let me go."

It was a long speech, and Gideon wondered if the Midianite was listening. It was the only way he could think of to save the flock and maybe—just maybe the lamb as well.

At last the Midianite spoke. "You are right. I am the son of our chief. It is true you could have done us more harm than you did. I suppose we owe you something for that. In a way we are equals. Your father is chief of your clan. My father is chief of the Midianites. I accept your challenge. There's a level place on top of the bank. We have our camels there. Two falls out of three."

The two boys scrambled up the bank together, followed by the other three. Gideon was thinking so much about the wrestling match to come that he hardly heard the question the Midianite asked. Turning to Gideon and pointing to the sling, he wanted to know, "Can you really send a stone to the mark every time with that thing?"

"As often as you hit the mark with that javelin," answered Gideon.

107

10

The Shepherd Brings His Flock Home

At one end of a narrow neck of land, four camels were hobbled. The ground was level enough. Gideon took off his cloak and tunic. He was clad only in coarse linen underpants, for he had removed his sandals. The Midianite removed headdress, outer cloak, and tunic. The two boys faced each other. For a moment they circled, each trying to find an advantage. Then they closed, each with his hands on the other's shoulders. Gideon tried to remember what he had seen his brother Lok do when he wrestled with Caleb. He was trying to think when he felt his feet go flying out from under him.

The Midianite had slipped one foot behind Gideon's, and a quick push had put Gideon on the ground. Quickly Gideon rolled aside just in time to avoid the Midianite's flying body. Gideon bounded to his feet and grabbed the leg of the other

boy. He was sure he had him now, but a sudden kick in the pit of his stomach made him turn loose and fall on his back. In an instant the Midianite was on top of him, pinning him firmly to the grass. Gideon had lost the first fall.

The two boys stood up and took a few deep breaths. The Midianite was smiling and confident now. Gideon's heart sank. He saw the lamb in the arms of the other young Midianite. He breathed deeply. Whatever happened he'd do his best.

His opponent came to him more quickly this time. The Midianite was anxious to press home his advantage and end the match. Gideon gave ground slowly as the Midianite pushed, looking for a chance to hook his leg around Gideon's. Gideon kept his eye on his opponent's right leg, always twisting sideways, so the left leg could not reach behind his own.

Slowly Gideon backed, when suddenly his heel came down on a loose stone, and he fell backwards. The Midianite was pushing with all his strength as Gideon fell heavily on the ground. At the last minute he managed to roll away. The Midianite hit the ground with a thump, face forward. Stunned for a moment by the heavy and unexpected fall, he was an easy victim. Gideon rolled him over and placed both knees on his chest. Now they had each won a fall. But something else had happened. Gideon had made a discovery. He had won by sheer luck, but he had learned something which could prove luckier than a loose stone.

Gideon helped the Midianite up and then searched out the loose stone on which his foot had slipped. He tossed it over into the wadi. Asking for time, he began to hunt through the grass for any other loose stones. He found two or three and tossed them away. The Midianites, curious about what he was doing, asked Gideon to explain. Soon all searched the grass for stones. A few more were found.

Now the Midianite seemed to have gotten over his annoyance at losing the second fall. He was more sure of himself than ever. Accidents couldn't happen twice in a row.

The third fall began. Again the Midianite closed eagerly. Now he was very confident and in more of a hurry than ever to end it. He pushed strongly and, just as before, Gideon gave ground grudgingly. The Midianite exerted all his strength, his foot searching for a misstep by Gideon which would allow his favorite maneuver. Gideon kept his eyes on his opponent's feet. As he felt the Midianite gather his strength for a hard push, he stiffened to meet the challenge. Suddenly Gideon sank backward to his knees. The Midianite, pushing with all his strength, sailed over Gideon's head. In a flash Gideon was on top of him, pinning him to the grass with his body. He had won! The lamb was safe!

Slowly the Midianite got to his feet. "It was a trick! You won by a trick! The first time it was an accident. I felt you stumble on the rock. This time you tricked me!" His eyes flashed, and there was a scowl on his face as he started toward Gideon.

Gideon stood his ground. Suddenly the Midianite stopped and laughed. "It was a trick, but it was fair. All that searching out the rocks. You wanted me to think it couldn't happen that way again, didn't you?"

Gideon nodded his head. "Yes, it was a trick. I wanted you

111

to think, with the stones out of the way, you had nothing to fear. You seemed to know more about wrestling than I. If I was going to save my lamb, it would have to be by a trick. Losing the lamb was my fault. There is never any excuse for a shepherd failing to watch his flock. If I hadn't practiced with your javelin, it might not have happened."

"I will keep my bargain, Manassite, for the word of a chief's son is to be respected. The lamb is yours and you are free to go."

The Midianite walked over to his comrade and took the lamb and gave it to Gideon.

"My name is Gideon. Keep your javelin. My sling is a better weapon for me. I know we can't be friends. Perhaps we'll never meet again, but I thank you for returning my lamb and keeping your word."

Gideon put on his clothes and took the lamb in his arms.

"My name is Oreb, which means raven—the fiercest of birds. I have a feeling we'll meet again someday, Gideon. If we do, I'll watch out for your tricks."

The Midianite too had slipped into his clothes and with his companions now turned toward the camels. Gideon, the lamb in his arms, hurried back toward his flock.

The sun was hanging low in the sky. He had lost much time looking for the lamb and then in the wrestling match. Only now did he become conscious of the bruise under his eye. It was beginning to hurt. There was a skinned place on one knee. But the lamb was safe. Now he must get to the flock.

Under Gideon's eye the bruise was beginning to swell. He

had gotten that on the first fall, when Oreb had thrown him —Oreb the raven. He wondered if they *would* meet again. It was possible, especially if the Midianites continued their almost yearly raiding. Gideon tried to move faster, but the lamb in his arms was heavy. He was going as fast as he could.

At last he saw a familiar sight, his cap. He was glad he had placed it there on his shepherd's staff. He hadn't really needed it for a guide mark, but it cheered him to see it and to know that he had almost reached his flock.

Gideon came up out of the wadi and was only a few yards from the flock before he saw the tall figure standing there. He moved cautiously, and then he recognized his brother Lok. Even the lamb in his arms couldn't hold him back now. He ran the last few steps. Lok looked down and lifted the lamb from Gideon's arms. He placed it next to the brown-faced ewe who, catching the scent of her lamb, moved anxiously forward.

"We worried for fear something had happened to you, younger brother. Had you not come in another minute, I would have come searching for you. But how could the lamb stray so far?"

Already the two brothers had started the flock on the homeward journey. "It's a long story, Lok. Maybe we'd better wait until we get home. I'll have to tell father anyway. When he hears, he may not trust me with the sheep again. I almost lost the lamb, and I could have lost the whole flock."

Gideon hurried to take the lead. Lok brought up the rear to make sure there were no strays. It was dark now, but the way was familiar, and the flock was safe. Gideon put a hand

114

up to the bruise under his eye, and a strange kind of contentment crept over him, tired as he was.

There were lamps burning in every house in Ophrah. The smell of charcoal cooking fires and food being prepared reached out to meet them as they neared the edge of the village. This night the evening meals were being eaten later than usual. All the villagers had worked late into the evening, finding their scattered belongings; bringing in food supplies they had left from the caves; repairing the damages caused by the Midianites.

Gideon paused at the low mud-walled enclosure adjoining his father's house. He opened the gate and Father Abraham marched through, leading the flock. When the last sheep passed through the gate, Gideon dropped the wooden latch. Now they were home—really home.

At the door of the house Joash and his wife, Leah, waited with Caleb. Gideon's mother brought the lamp in her hand close to Gideon's face and cried out at the bruise she saw there. The skin had turned dark and was so swollen the eye was nearly shut.

"I can see you must have a story to tell, Gideon," said Joash, watching as his wife applied a soft cloth dipped in cool water to her youngest son's cheek. "But first we'll give thanks that all of us are here together and safe, and eat our evening meal. Then you can tell us what happened today.

"The Lord is my strength and my song,
    and he has become my salvation;

115

this is my God, and I will praise him,
    my father's God, and I will exalt him."*

The strong voice of Joash pronounced the words and the rest listened in silence with bowed heads. As Joash finished, the others raised their heads. Joash looked at the three small birds on the plate in the center of the table. They were roasted a golden brown and the smell was delicious.

"You're not the only one who uses the sling with skill, Gideon. Thanks to the sure eye of your brother Caleb and his new sling, we're eating well tonight. Your brother brought down three rock-pigeons in the foothills of Mount Ebal. They're as tasty as partridge and a welcome change from the diet of the cave."

Tonight there were lentils, barley bread, and a thin cake made with barley flour, honey, and crushed walnuts. The rock-pigeons had been roasted over the earthen charcoal brazier. The flesh was brown and crisp. Tonight there was no wine—even for Joash. The Midianites had seen to that. Goat's milk had to do. Still it was a meal which seemed like a feast after the frugal fare of the cave.

"Now," said Joash brushing the last crumbs from his beard, "let me hear your story, Gideon. It's plain you had some kind of adventure."

All eyes turned to Gideon. He felt a sinking feeling coming over him. What if his father would not trust him to lead the

*Exodus 15:2.

flock to pasture again? No more days with Father Abraham? He had to begin. It couldn't be helped.

"We made our way down the mountain, Father Abraham, the flock, and I. It was well into morning and I turned the flock east toward the small meadow that borders the wadi. It's farther from the village than most of the pastures, and I was sure the other flocks would pasture nearer the village. This meant our flock would have the pasture to themselves. Now that I think back, it was too late to start for that pasture. I should have stayed nearer the village. I didn't think of it at the time.

"We reached the pasture and the grass was good as it always is there. I had taken with me the javelin Caleb took from the Midianite. I began to practice throwing the javelin at a tree branch I set up as a target. I must not have watched the flock as I should have, for when I checked I saw at once that a lamb was missing. There was nothing to do but huddle the flock and hope Father Abraham would keep them together until I returned. I had to go find the lamb.

"First I searched toward the village but the lamb was not there. Then I began to search east down the wadi. Where the meadow borders the wadi, the bank is low. The lamb could easily have gone down the bank and wandered down the dry creek bed. I walked for a long time. Now I realize I walked farther than it would have been possible for the lamb to stray, but I didn't think of it then. There's a place where the bank on the opposite side is very high and the near side bank is only shoulder level.

"It was here the Midianites jumped down from the bank

on the near side. There were four of them. I was frightened and I didn't know what to do. Two of them were about the size of Lok. The other two were those Caleb and I had seen in the wheat field. The richly dressed one is a chief's son, Caleb. His name is Oreb. The word means raven in their tongue.

"The chief's son, the one named Oreb, taunted me. I forgot I was afraid and let him know that it was Caleb and I who had turned their camels loose and chased them away. Oreb asked a lot of questions. He finally found out how Father and Lok captured the four Midianites and tied them to trees.

"Oreb threatened to go back and kill all the sheep in our flock and even kill me. I wasn't sure he meant to do all that. But he was very angry. He said they had watched me bring the flock into the pasture. One of his men had slipped the lamb away while I was practicing with the javelin. They knew I would follow to find the lamb, so they hid and waited for me to come looking for it.

"I was certain they would kill the lamb at least or take it away with them. I knew there was nothing I could do against the four of them. Then I got an idea. I reminded the chief's son we could have killed their camels, but we only chased them out of the wheat. I told them my father and Lok could have killed the men they captured instead of just tying them up. Caleb could have even killed Oreb and Hanun—that's the other one's name. Then I proposed we settle the dispute ourselves—just the two of us.

"I challenged him to wrestle. The one who won two falls out of three would be the winner. If he won, I would return

118

the javelin, give him my sling, and let him keep the lamb. If I won, he would give me back the lamb and let me go free. I guess he thought he could beat me easily. Anyway, he agreed to the wrestling match.

"He won the first fall quickly. I was trying to remember what Lok does when he wrestles with Caleb. It all happened so quickly I couldn't remember anything. That's when I got the bruise under my eye. I won the next fall by an accident. Oreb was pushing with all his might, and I was backing up when my heel slipped on a stone. I fell backwards. Oreb sailed over my head, and I got on top of him before he could get up.

"This gave me an idea. I pretended to search for all the stones in the grass and throw them out of the way. When we wrestled for the third time, I waited until Oreb was pushing as hard as he could. Then I dropped backwards to my knees, and he went over my head. He was so surprised that I was able to get on top of him before he could recover. Slipping on the stone made me think of it. Otherwise he would have beaten me.

"Oreb was mad at first, but even if it was a trick he knew it was fair. So he kept his word, gave me back the lamb, and let me go." Gideon stopped, out of breath and sure that his father would be angry because he had failed to watch the flock closely.

"So, the flock is safe and you are home." Joash's voice was solemn. "But what if they had already killed the lamb when they stopped you? What if the chief's son had not been willing to accept your challenge? And what if you had lost the wrestling match?"

"I know, Father. A shepherd never takes his eyes from his

flock. If you can trust me again to lead the flock, I'll never do something else when I should be watching the sheep." Gideon looked his father in the eye and did not turn his head when Joash returned his look.

"You must remember a shepherd always leads his flock and protects them. I think you know that, now. You have learned something else, Gideon. To fight is not always a bad thing. There are times when we must fight." Joash's voice took on a sterner tone, and he seemed to be talking to himself instead of his son.

"You did well. You are the best thinker of us all. You'll lead our sheep, Gideon. They know your voice and now they know you will protect them and keep them safe."

Joash smiled at his youngest son. With his one good eye, Gideon smiled happily back.

And Afterwards

The young man was tall and well muscled. He might have been nineteen. How quickly he had grown these last few years! It seemed almost overnight the boy had become a man—ready to take his place with his older brothers. The sweat rolled down his face. Beating out the wheat heads with a heavy club was hot work in the close, still air of the winepress.

To one unfamiliar with the circumstances, it would have seemed odd to find a man threshing wheat by hand in the sunken winepress. Wheat was usually threshed on a wide flat open place where the wind could separate chaff from grain. Often a threshing sledge was used instead of threshing by hand. Why did this man thresh wheat by hand in a secret place? It was the old reason—to thresh and store even a small part of the crop before it was taken by the Midianites. A man needed to find a safe hiding place when he lived in the land of the Manasseh.

It was hot and the chaff from the wheat stuck to Gideon's neck and scratched his face and arms. As he paused to wipe the sweat from his eyes, he noticed a man sitting beneath the oak tree opposite the winepress. The man watched him as he worked. Gideon turned a questioning look toward the man and heard the stranger speak.

"The Lord is with you, O mighty man of courage."

Gideon, wondering if the man mocked him, answered, "Sir, if the Lord is really with us, why have all these things happened to us? Where are all the great deeds we have been told about? Why have we been handed over to the Midianites?" His heart as heavy as before, Gideon turned back to the task of beating the grains from the wheat.

Again the man spoke and stood close to Gideon. "Go in your strength and deliver the people of Manasseh from the Midianites who invade your land. Am I not the one who summons you?"

Gideon lay down his threshing club. "Sir, my clan is the weakest in Manasseh, and I am the least in my father's household."

Even as he answered, Gideon knew the person to whom he spoke was no ordinary man. The words old Joel had spoken so long ago came back to him again. "Joshua knew well enough when God spoke to him through a messenger." Could it really be so?

Once more the stranger spoke: "But it is I who will stand

with you. You, and those whom you gather with you, shall strike the Midianites as one man."

"If the Lord has truly chosen me, show me a sign that it is Yahweh who speaks to me. Stay and let me bring a gift to you."

Gideon left his threshing and went to his house where he prepared a young goat. With this offering of meat, he brought also cakes of unleavened barley bread when he returned. These simple things were the best that he owned. He offered them to the man. Surely, he felt, this must be a messenger from God.

The stranger told Gideon to put the meat and barley cakes on a rock near the oak tree and to pour the broth from the meat over them. As Gideon did this, the stranger touched the meat and barley cakes with the tip of his staff. At once a fire blazed up and completely consumed the food.

Gideon knew now he was face to face with a messenger from God. He fell on his knees and cried out in fear and wonder. "Alas, O Yahweh, I have seen your messenger!"

But before the stranger left Gideon, he told him not to be afraid. He would be protected. So Gideon built a stone altar beneath the oak tree and called it "a place of peace."

There were other tests for Gideon and other commands. In the end he had no doubts, for he remembered still other words of Joel. "One can only be sure of winning when he knows Yahweh, the one true God, is on his side. There must always be a sign from God." Gideon received a sign from God and followed the commands of his messenger.

There was evidence that Gideon was a thoughtful leader

who planned well. Of a great number of men from Ophrah and the other villages he chose only a few. He chose those who were most vigilant and alert. These were to be Yahweh's men—men who would act as one man to defeat the Midianites.

Gideon did fight the Midianites. He did free the people of Israel. And afterwards the words of his own father, spoken long ago, came back to his memory. "You'll lead our sheep, Gideon. They know your voice and they know, now, that you will protect them and keep them safe."

FIRST CHRISTIAN CHURCH
1500 North Mississippi
LITTLE ROCK, ARKANSAS